D   night

Book One of the Immortal
Kindred Series

Clara Winter

To Shelley, Wonderful to meet you
Clara Winter

The characters and events in this book are fictitious. Any similarity to real persons, living or dead, places, or events is coincidental and not intended by the author.

If you purchase this book without a cover you should be aware that this book may have been stolen property and reported as "unsold and destroyed" to the publisher. In such case the author has not received any payment for this "stripped book."

Deepest Midnight
Copyright © 2018 Clara Winter
All rights reserved.

ISBN: (ebook): 978-1-945910-64-7
(print): 978-1-945910-83-8

Inkspell Publishing
5764 Woodbine Ave.
Pinckney, MI 48169

Edited By Shelly Small
Cover art By Najla Qamber

This book, or parts thereof, may not be reproduced in any form without permission. The copying, scanning, uploading, and distribution of this book via the internet or via any other means without the permission of the publisher is illegal and punishable by law. Please purchase only authorized electronic or print editions, and do not participate in or encourage piracy of copyrighted materials. Your support of the author's rights is appreciated.

DEDICATION

To Brian--my love throughout the ages
and Quinn--my life's inspiration

CLARA WINTER

CHAPTER ONE

Mourning lost love is no way to spend your existence. However, this is what I have done for over two hundred years.

I sit cross-legged on the velvet loveseat, elbows on my knees and chin cupped in my hands. Sitting still is impossible. I'm jittery, something I've been a lot lately. Alexandre, my maker and companion, is occupied with his tablet next to me. Through the dimly lit living room, I can barely make out the white scrollwork of the ornate ceiling medallion. Flames roar in the cavernous fireplace, despite the outdoor temperature of ninety-seven degrees. It should be a cozy scene. Instead, I drop my face into my hands and lower my head.

"Go be miserable somewhere else, Millicent," grumbles Alexandre.

It's going to be one of those nights. Alexandre pulls me up and hands me my black leather clutch. He steers me toward the darkly stained front door of our antebellum Savannah home. Before opening the door, he bends down to put shoes on my feet, like I'm a child. If he wants me to brood elsewhere, I will. Alexandre values bright and cheerful people. His reason for tolerating my presence for so long is one of life's many mysteries.

"We have all lost people we love, Mills. We go on. If you can't ever learn to do the same, what's the point?"

"Good question, what is the point?"

Alexandre taps me on the nose. "You can choose to be happy again. I'm not sure how much longer I can stand to have you around like this. For tonight, go find something to distract your mind."

I can't blame Alexandre for wanting me to disappear. The life of the party tires of the buzz kill. Thankfully, one of the many wonderful things about Savannah is the abundance of mysterious locales, all perfect for sulking. Secluded squares, thick with foliage dripping in Spanish moss, decaying alleyways lined with ancient cobblestone, and hidden stone staircases topped with wrought iron railings--all perfect places to hide away. My stormy mood has long felt at home in this haunted city.

My immortal sister, Annie, says you only get one true love. If her saying is true, then I was out of luck before I ever became immortal. Eternity is a long time when you have no hope of ever finding happiness again. And Alexandre wonders why I'm so melancholy all the time. He seems to have no concept of despair. Grief has this insidious way of winding itself around your heart and never letting go.

I decide the best place for a sulky girl craving diversion is a nice, crowded bar. The muggy June evening is already warming me up. The extremely humid heat has long been a friend to my frigid body temperature.

It's midnight when my Louboutin's hit Congress Street. The area is typically urban with businesses lining the paved streets. Loud music, mostly jazz, pours out of clubs and restaurants. Along the sidewalk, cars are parked. In addition, dozens of other cars drive by slowly, hoping against hope to find a spot of their own.

A young, very drunk man is on the prowl. He yells at a pretty young woman crossing the street. "Hey, gorgeous!" She doesn't look back but makes it safely across the busy road, into the cocoon of waiting friends. Just another typical Friday night.

I blend into the crowd, another over privileged girl out for a good time. Skinny jeans and a t-shirt help me look like everyone else. It's hard though, to shake the proper posture of nobility. My black eyes scan the people on the street. It would be so easy to pick one to use to my heart's content. In the 1700's, I was almost freakishly tall at 5'9", but not anymore. Now my height and slender figure are considered sexy. Maybe in a hundred years, I'll look like a freak again.

The life on Congress is a good distraction. Maybe a different distraction will do. It has been a while. I've noticed several mortals eyeing me up and down. Shamelessly taking in everything with their eyes. No need to be coy in this era. I spot a tall, dark-haired Goth staring right at me. I take his measure, as I start to walk by.

He steps in front of me. "Maybe I can help you find whatever it is you're looking for."

He's handsome, but his eyes have a leering quality which creeps me out. A mashup of lust and maliciousness reminds me of two men I would rather not think of. I'm suddenly overcome with disgust, continuing right past him.

Deciding this isn't for me, after all, I keep walking. A couple of blocks down, I turn right, heading for River Street. My new destination is the riverfront. The soothing sound of rushing water calms me. Perhaps being alone isn't the best idea, but my options are limited. This restlessness is making me indecisive, which can be dangerous for mortals crossing my path.

The streets are quiet. Every other step or so, my foot sends a few small, black cockroaches scurrying. Creatures of the night, like myself. In the relative silence, my unhappiness hits me again. Alexandre has told me many times how vampires go through emotional ups and downs, just like humans. He says it passes eventually. According to Alexandre, vampires just feel things more deeply and because we live forever, a depressive episode can last for years. I think he's being optimistic. In 240 years, I've never seen Alexandre sad for long. The hard truth is after this long I feel the sadness will never leave me. Drastic measures may have to be taken at some point.

River Street is my home away from home. Uneven cobblestone underfoot, shops and restaurants to my right, trees and black, smooth water to my left. After walking about halfway down, I notice camera crews. For the last couple of days, I have seen them around. Areas of town are sectioned off with bright industrial lighting, trailers, and curious onlookers. A movie is being filmed but I haven't been all that interested.

Alexandre, on the other hand, loves movies. He is besotted with the dark-haired beauty starring in this film. His mission is to meet and seduce her, which I'm sure he will. At 6'3", Alexandre is all male, with a face that could have been chiseled from marble and a perfect, wicked smile. He is blond with baby-blue eyes. His muscular body could very easily sell underwear any day of the week.

He is happy to bounce from one bed to the next, sating his very healthy appetite for female flesh. And why shouldn't he have his fun? He's the very copy of a Roman god, and women can't help but fall over themselves to please him. Annie and I, are seemingly the only two women able to resist his charms.

I reach into my clutch to take out my phone. Someone may as well get lucky tonight. Before I can begin my text, Alexandre is next to me. Being psychically linked to him stinks sometimes. Ok, all the time. If I wasn't so lazy, I would learn how to shield my thoughts.

I put my phone away. He says, "You know I hate texting."

"Why are you whispering? Who could possibly hear us?" I ask, in my sweetest southern belle accent. Irritating him is what I do best, although he doesn't always take the bait.

"Do you see her?" He pauses, looking around. "There she is in the back, next to the man with the copper hair. Don't you have a thing for gingers, Mills?" He tugs on my arm, pointing with his other hand, as I look up.

Alexandre starts explaining how he is going to approach her. I roll my eyes. He thinks he can just walk up to a world-famous movie star, throw up an eyebrow, and she'll be stripping naked. The annoying thing is, she probably will. On the last half of my eye roll, I lock eyes with a man who was murdered over two hundred years ago. All the breath leaves my body.

CHAPTER TWO

"What is it Mills? Do you know that man? He looks familiar," Alexandre asks as he tugs at my arm again.

Without answering, I pull away from him, spinning around. I have no idea where I'm going, but my head is swimming. If it was at all possible for me to faint, I'd face plant into the uneven cobblestone. I walk fast, but not too fast. It's important to maintain the appearance I'm just another mortal experiencing a late night, drunken crisis.

Taking deep breaths, I try to order my thoughts. For one thing, it isn't possible. It can't be him. Blood tears fill my eyes, but I fight them back. It wouldn't do to be seen with bloody streaks running down my face. Talk about a terrifying scene for a mortal to witness.

Once I know I'm out of sight, I stop for a minute and put my head against the cool brick of a restaurant wall. I need to calm down. My long blonde hair falls out of my bun, spilling around my face.

Looking back toward the river, I notice Alexandre couldn't be bothered to follow me. Obviously, my emotional welfare takes a back seat when he's on the prowl. Which is fine with me. He'd only bother me, at least that's what I tell myself.

Maybe I should go back to have another look. Just a quick glance around the corner.

Just because I'm immortal, doesn't mean my mind can't play tricks on me. I've been sullen, obsessively thinking of him nonstop. It makes perfect sense that my troubled mind would manifest him or someone who resembles him. Any psychiatrist would agree with me. The fact he was quite singular in appearance, would mean nothing to a mind that has been as emotionally disturbed as mine of late.

I decide not to go back to the riverfront. Best to wait and collect myself before I stalk this man. I'm going to become like all the women Alexandre has ever slept with and brushed off. I could slap myself.

"You ok, honey? Can I call someone for you?"

I feel the light pressure of a female hand on my back.

"I'm fine, thanks. Just a little dizzy."

I dare not turn around to look the woman in the face. I can still feel the blood pooling in my eyes.

"Let me call you an Uber, or something."

"No, thank you, my house is just a couple of blocks from here."

I circle around the well-meaning woman, keeping my face turned away. Better to be rude than traumatize her for life.

I feel an urgent need to head home. Doubling back half a block, I walk straight up Drayton, passing a lovely mixture of Victorian and Colonial style homes. I hoof it back to Forsyth Park, which our house faces. Completely zoned out, I keep my head down. If there are other people around me, I take no notice. I'm calmer, although my mind still reels. Hopefully, Annie will be at the house. She'll know what to do.

I was the first of Alexandre's fledglings. After I had been turned, we left France for the exciting city of Colonial Boston, where I met Annie one night in a pub. The girl had such fire, such personality, I couldn't help but be drawn to her. For someone who had always been in the shadow of one man or another, she was dazzling. I soon learned her secret. Annie, a woman, was aiding the rebellion against the English. I introduced her to Alexandre, and shortly thereafter, she became one of us.

Neither of us knows much about Alexandre's life before France. He always says it isn't worth talking about. Maybe it isn't to him, but I have always been curious to know more. He won't even disclose his true age.

DEEPEST MIDNIGHT

Now on Whitaker, but still across the street, I can see the house is completely lit up. Annie is the only one who turns on every light in the house. I breathe a sigh of relief for the first time in twenty minutes.

Our stately Victorian has been here since before the Civil War and is very popular with tourists. The pale-yellow house, with black shutters and two stacked porches which run the entire width of the home, has been ours for about thirty years.

Walking up the steps, the smell of fresh blood hits me. Then I hear Annie's high-pitched laughter. Of course, Annie is entertaining, I shouldn't have expected anything less. When my friend brings a man to the house, she usually makes sure there is enough for both of us. She says I don't eat enough these days, and she's right. Currently, I'm famished, feeling immediately grateful to Annie for going to the trouble. Not that attracting men is any trouble for my gorgeous friend.

The solid oak door swings wide, framing my rebel immortal in all her glory. No one would dare call Annie plain. Her voluptuous beauty helped her tremendously as she manipulated her way through various high-ranking officers of the English army. She was quite skilled at extracting secrets, then passing them on to the Culper Spy Ring. She is fearless and fierce, always standing up for what is right.

Annie stands in the doorway with the light from the hallway silhouetting her from behind. Her auburn hair tumbles around her in loose curls, her lovely almond shaped brown eyes are shining. Her petite figure carries breasts I would kill for. If anyone can snag two willing guys off the street, it's this girl.

"There you are. I have someone who is dying to meet you," she puts the emphasis on dying, because vampire humor is our thing. "Wait, something's up. If you weren't already dead, I'd say you look like death warmed over."

"Something is up in the worst way. I need to talk to you, now."

"Can it wait until after we've eaten?" Annie grins wickedly.

"Only if it's a quick bite," I quip back.

"Cute, you win this round. I was hoping to take my time this evening, but for you, anything."

Annie takes my hand, pulls me inside, and then slams the door. The door is over a hundred years old, slamming it drives Alexandre crazy. She leads me into the living room, and is the first one to speak, "Sam, this is the hot blonde I was telling you about."

Sam extends his hand, a drunken smile on his lips. I take it, pulling him into me so we are eye to eye. Behind me, I know Annie is doing the same. No words are necessary, it only takes a second to mesmerize him. The moment I'm sure he is in my power, I bend his head to the side, sinking my fangs into his soft flesh. The warm, iron taste of Sam's blood gushes into my mouth, sliding down my throat. It takes only moments to drink enough to slake my thirst, but not enough to take his life. Make no mistake, I'm not innocent. I've taken life before on several occasions and even enjoyed it. Just because we try to avoid killing doesn't mean we aren't monsters. We are monsters, we just like to keep a low profile.

After I release Sam, Annie comes over, taking his arm. Both men are still in la-la land. Annie will lead them a few blocks away where they will come to, having no idea what happened. Judging by the way Sam tasted, they were three sheets to the wind a while ago. They will, no doubt, attribute their disorientation to being drunk and call it a night. Everyone wins.

Annie comes back, dropping her lovely self onto the plush velvet sofa.

"Ok, spill," she says.

I perch on the loveseat. "I saw him, Annie. I saw Julien." No point in beating around the bush.

"Come again? Julien, the legendary lover from your past? That Julien?" She thinks I've finally lost it.

"He's the one. I locked eyes with him not twenty minutes ago on the riverfront. He was on a film set."

"Mills, my love. He died, right? You saw him murdered right in front of you. Are you positive it was the same man? I mean, it's been over two hundred years. Maybe it was just someone who resembles Julien."

This is exactly what I need to hear. Thank you, Annie, for being the voice of reason.

"I don't know the answer, and no, I never saw Julien's body. It could be a strong resemblance, or he could be a descendant of Julien's. There's also the possibility, it *is* him. You and I have certainly witnessed some pretty strange things over the centuries. Look at us, we exist. I can't just leave this alone." I give her the best sad eyes I can muster.

DEEPEST MIDNIGHT

Annie bites her lip and looks at the floor. This is what she always does when she is considering her options. It's adorable, and she knows it.

"Ok, the first thing we have to do is get you in front of this guy," she finally says.

This is one of the many amazing things about Annie. I can count on her to step up to the plate. But, before Annie can come up with a plan, I slam my face into the palm of my hand.

"Something you want to share, Mills?"

"Alexandre is on a mission to score with the star of this movie. I think her name is Kathryn Hart?"

"Yep, that sounds like Alexandre. And, of course he will."

"Exactly. When has Alexandre never succeeded at winning a conquest? He may be my best shot at meeting mystery guy face to face," I reason.

As if on cue, my phone buzzes. I put it to my ear.

"I know you hate it when I talk through your head. There is no way this guy is who you think he is."

"Alexandre," I sigh.

"Just a minute. I was going to add I've made the acquaintance of the ravishing Ms. Hart. She and her friends have been invited to our home tomorrow night for cocktails. In case you need help figuring it out, one of her friends is what's his name. I admit the resemblance is troubling, but it can only be coincidence."

"Alexandre, you are my favorite male-endowed vampire. And it isn't troubling, it's exciting."

"Uh-huh."

"Don't be grumpy."

"I'm just hoping that one day you will get over this foolishness and look who's talking. The guy seems like kind of a snob, which I know you hate. Hopefully, he treats you like garbage, so we can finally put the ghost of Julien to rest."

"Gee, thanks dad."

I hit end and toss my phone on the table. Alexandre hates it when I call him dad. Which is exactly why I do it whenever he makes me angry.

"What was that about?" asks Annie politely, even though she heard Alexandre's every word.

"Our maker is bringing over some playmates tomorrow," I say, winking.

"Leave it to the brawny Frenchman to score so quickly. Is one of these so-called playmates the guy you want to play with?" she asks, raising an eyebrow.

"Yes, Ma'am. What are your plans for the rest of the night?" I ask.

"My plan is to make sure you have a kick-ass outfit all ready to go for tomorrow's party."

After Annie leaves me for the night, I settle into the silky, white sheets of my decadent four-poster bed. After today's revelations, it would be impossible not to think of the past. Thoughts and images buried long ago struggle to the surface. Most are not pleasant to reconsider, although there were glimmers of light and hope.

***

Winter 1772, Burgundy Region, France

Our wedding night is spent at an inn, halfway to my new home. I blame my shaking on the cold, but in truth, I feel like I could be sick. I met Charles only once before today. He is handsome enough, a tall man with chestnut hair, hazel eyes, and only a slight paunch. Underneath the well-groomed exterior, I sense a severe personality which makes me nervous.

"I'll step out while you undress and get into bed. Try to be quick, I'm tired."

There is nothing I can do but follow his instructions.

Taking deep breaths and trying not to vomit, I unbutton my black cloak. Folding it neatly, I place it on the chair next to the plain, wooden bed. I step out of my blue satin travelling gown and place it in the same manner on top of my cloak. I remain in my cream-colored silk shift, and climb under the covers, pulling them up to my chin.

Mercifully, it is over quickly and with only a little pain. Charles is mostly gentle, but he makes no attempt to inspire any passion in me.

"We will make lovely children," he murmurs, before rolling off me and falling asleep. I think about being used as a vessel, night after night, and cry myself softly to sleep.

The dream opens outside a grand chateau, three times the size of my father's. In the light of the full moon, I can make out the creamy yellow tint of stone, and French blue shutters. The length of the building seems to go on forever. I can't help but marvel at the rows upon rows of windows.

Oddly, I feel comfortable. I know where I am and feel no fear. I turn automatically, walking toward a path. The path is barely visible, at the very edge of the grounds, leading into the forest. I stop, peering into the dense wood. This is the way, I know it.

I walk for almost an hour. Just when I think the path will go on and on, it abruptly ends.

Before me is a small clearing with a tiny stone cabin in the center. Smoke creeps from the chimney. Cords of firewood sit, stacked under the front window. As I move toward the rounded, wooden door, it opens. Stepping into the doorway is Jupiter, the Roman God. At least, that's who I fancy he is. I see him perfectly in the moonlight, which glints off his crystal clear, blue eyes. He is very tall and muscular, with shoulder length, honey-blond hair. His eyes should be cold, but they are warm and full of love.

Jupiter opens his arms. I run into them, bursting into tears.

"I know, my child. Cry all you like. You are safe and loved, just wait, wait," he says, softly against my hair. He holds me, gently swaying us back and forth.

"Wait for what?"

"To come away with me."

"Why must I wait? I'm ready now. Please don't make me go back," I whisper into his shirt, now wet with my tears.

"Not yet, you are still too young."

I pull away, starting to feel angry, "I'm not too young to be married and bear the children of a man I despise."

"In my mind, you are certainly too young to bear children. I have something for you."

Jupiter disappears into the dark recess of the cabin, leaving me on the stoop. Returning, he places a small cloth bag in my hand.

"This is a tea. Brew a cup and drink it every time your husband leaves your bed. It will prevent him from getting a child in you. Hide it well."

I grip the bag, greedily, "How will I get more?"

"I will replenish it. You needn't worry. You are special, Millicent. I will be watching, don't be afraid."

I wake with a start from the dream feeling warm, like a child stepping out of her father's loving embrace. An embrace, I just now felt for the first time. In my hand is the cloth bag. It is natural that it should be there. I slip soundlessly from the bed and tuck it into the back of my jewelry case.

CLARA WINTER

CHAPTER THREE

I wake musing on my once mortal dreams of Alexandre. He was my saving grace. Attending my wedding on the arm of a young French Duchess, he saw me for the first time, feeling an immediate kinship. I have Alexandre to thank for everything.

The sun is setting, and I have butterflies in my stomach. I'm hoping to get some answers tonight.

Leaning up on an elbow, I pull open the thick, black velvet curtains which surround my bed. I slide out of the silk sheets, bracing myself against one of the bedposts. Since becoming immortal, I've never suffered such a case of nerves.

I shuffle across the cold, hard floors and open the light tight shutter attached to the street facing window. I love this room, my sanctuary. The silver Chinoiserie wallpaper, printed with swallows, and the heavy, substantial whitewashed furniture, was all chosen by me. Oddly enough, I tend to choose items which remind me of the life I once lived. My mortal life may not have been ideal, but there's no denying the beauty of those former surroundings.

Opening the window, I stick my head out, breathing in the lovely fragrance of the gardenias. It's a feast for the senses. The beauty of the varied architecture, the foliage, music and food, combine to make Savannah a perfect place for the joyful and brooding alike.

One would think such a place always smells of flowers and mossy trees. At times, however, it is also possible to detect the underlying odor of decay. Old buildings and a high level of moisture in the air, do not mix well. You take the good with the bad, I guess. I can hear laughter, a young woman singing an unfamiliar song, and a trumpet being played in Forsyth Park. This is the south, after all, where music is as natural as the humid heat. The large city park is always a center of tourist and local activity, with the famous Forsyth Park Fountain holding down the north end.

"What are you up to? Excited for tonight?" Annie asks, poking her head through the door.

"I'm more nervous than excited," I pause. "Do you think it's really possible?"

"Anything is possible. I just don't want you to be disappointed, Mills. Why don't we surf the web, see what we can find out about this past life stuff?"

I kick myself. "You're a genius. Why didn't I think of that last night?"

"You were a bit preoccupied," Annie says, flopping on my bed.

Sitting down next to her, I pull my tablet from the nightstand drawer for a quick search on reincarnation.

The first thing I see is a string of pop quizzes to help me uncover my past lives. I can't help but wonder if I will find out that I was once Cleopatra, or perhaps even, Joan of Arc. I doubt these tests ever reveal the taker was once a bored housewife, or a cashier at the local drugstore. At this point, I would gladly take bored housewife. At least it would have meant, I have someone to love and care for me.

"Ooh, click on that one. Who do you think I would be?" Annie sits behind me, resting her chin on my shoulder.

"Marquis de Sade?" I tease her.

"Very funny, look who's talking." She butts my back with her chest.

We learn a couple of interesting things right off the bat. It seems there may be several indicators for having lived a past life; déjà vu, recurring dreams, attraction to specific places and time periods. Maybe there will be some way for me to steer the conversation into one of these topics this evening, but how would that go?

"Excuse me, man who looks like Julien, do you ever find yourself dreaming of chateaus, portrait painting, and murder?" He would think me deranged.

"Look at this one, Annie. This man claims when a soul is reincarnated, there can be similarities to the former self. For the most part, however, the new individual develops their own separate personality. Thus, becoming a completely new person, with only echoes of the old soul. I wonder what the point of reincarnation is then, when there is little similarity to the former self." I frown at the tablet.

Maybe my mystery man is Julien reincarnated, but with a wholly different personality. He could be completely odious, a sadistic freak, or a wonderful human. The possibilities are endless. I also have no idea if he is even single or straight. This could be my second chance at love, or it could be a complete disaster.

"We've researched for all of five minutes. This gives us a starting place and more for you to explore tonight," Annie says, still sitting up behind me.

"I know. Right now, we need to get moving. It's 8:30 which means I only have an hour until the cocktail party."

"I'm sure you want to take a bath, I'll check in with you later." She bounces off the bed.

Alexandre shared that there will be eight people in attendance this evening. Seven too many, in my opinion. My mystery man is apparently a character actor whose name Alexandre forgot. I refuse to call him Julien, even in my head.

Before getting ready for the night, I decide to head out to feed. The fresh blood will give me a little color and keep me from wanting to attack our guests, which isn't very neighborly. I pull on my uniform of skinny jeans, black heels, and a fresh, slouchy black tee. Heading downstairs, I notice Alexandre must have gone out already. No doubt he plans on pulling out all the stops to impress his ladylove this evening.

I don't want to be bothered with any nonsense tonight, so I go with what I know is easy. I stroll a few blocks past the park, sauntering along until I see a woman walking alone in Calhoun Square, which is otherwise deserted. Historic homes and magnolia trees line the space, with a little patch of green and a couple of benches at its center. Like all the squares in this area, it is lovely and charming and tends to put people at ease when they should always be slightly on guard.

This woman has no idea what easy prey she is. Luckily for her, I have no plans to do any lasting harm. As she is about to walk past me, I stop and turn her, pulling up her chin so she must consider my eyes. The young blonde starts to protest but is quickly mesmerized once our eyes meet. I push her into a doorway, lifting her up as I press myself against her. Tilting her head, I drink quickly. At first glance, should anyone come along, we will look like two lovers making out, but best not to be too risky. I finish with her and walk back the way I came.

The bite marks will heal instantly, so there is no need to worry about her remembering our encounter. Don't ask me the science behind it, because I have no idea. Chalk it up to another thing I never cared enough to learn. All I know is that our blood heals, and a drop or two of vampire blood will quickly heal the small puncture wounds caused by our fangs. If one is careful not to spill any blood, the victims come back to reality within several minutes, feeling dizzy, but no worse for wear. No harm, no foul.

Walking back home with her sweet blood moving through me, I feel a sense of excitement, even hope. These feelings have long eluded me, and it feels wonderful. Perhaps one day soon, the heavy weight of perpetual sadness will be lifted entirely.

Once I turn left onto E. Gaston, two blocks from my house, I sense Alexandre there. I pick up the pace, curious to see what he has purchased for the evening's festivities. Three of the eight guests won't be able to ingest any food, which of course means that he will have bought out the market, just so he can put out a ridiculous spread.

From outside the house, I glimpse Alexandre through the window, bustling about. I don't tell him enough, but I am grateful to have him. He took me under his wing when I was a wreck of a human being. Hell bent on destruction, I was not a pleasant person. Alexandre worked the change and then allowed me to be as destructive as I wished. Afterwards, he cared for and sheltered me.

I walk into the kitchen where Alexandre is unloading his bounty.

"What's on the menu tonight?" I ask.

"You look almost, dare I say, happy?" He narrows his eyes at me.

"Don't start. How can I help?"

"You can prepare the charcuterie board if you don't mind. I'm going to cut up fruit for the cocktails."

I'm impressed. Alexandre intends for the food to be understated and elegant. I cut up cheeses, bread, and meats, arranging them on the board. Lastly, I put some olives and fig preserves in small bowls, also for the board.

"Nicely done, Mills. It's almost nine and I'm sure you would like plenty of time to get ready. I've got the rest."

I feel like I'm being dismissed but must admit he's right. I bound up the stairs, two at a time.

In my four-piece bathroom surrounded by gray marble and chrome, I strip off my clothes, tossing them in the wicker hamper. My vintage 1885 claw foot bathtub, one of the first of its kind, fills with hot water. I add my favorite lavender-scented French bubble bath. The room quickly becomes hot and steamy which I find comforting.

I've never been someone who enjoys being cold, even though as a vampire, we invariably always run in that direction. I'll take hot and steamy, over frigid any day. I dip myself into the steaming water, then slide down until only my head is visible. Closing my eyes, I take a precious moment to relax.

With my eyes closed, I see Julian standing in front of me as if it was yesterday. With a somewhat crooked nose, my Julien was not a conventional example of male beauty, and his burnt-ochre colored hair was rare for a Frenchman. But, it was his eyes. The intense, deep-blue eyes were always the focus of my gaze. Not to mention his lean, hard body.

Julien's voice only added to his sex appeal. He spoke quietly in a deep, husky voice. Every time he spoke, all the females in his vicinity would immediately give him their full attention. Myself included.

As I'm toweling off, the door opens.

"Come on in, Annie. Why bother knocking?"

She ignores me and sits on the edge of the tub.

"I'm doing your hair, so get dry and throw on a robe. For a French, noble woman who knew Marie Antoinette, you would think you would have hair styling down." It was true. A ponytail was usually as fancy as I got with my hair.

"You know that's because I never did my own hair, right?"

"Of course, your majesty." She bows, mockingly.

"It's my lady, but whatever." I snap her with my towel, while we laugh.

I notice Annie is wearing a cute, but formless navy blue, shift style dress with a high neck. She's a good friend to let me shine tonight.

Annie works her magic and my hair looks stunning. Brushing the blonde strands until they shine, she then styles the dazzling threads into a chic chignon up-do. We keep my makeup light and fresh. I hate heavy makeup, always have.

"I love it. You should get me ready every night."

"Sure, I don't have anything better to do, my lady," she says sarcastically, playfully pinching my arm. "Let's get you in that dress."

She pulls a black lace push-up bra and matching black lace seamless panties out of a drawer and passes them to me. Thongs are not my undergarments of choice. Taking the dress, she found hiding in the back of my armoire last night, off its hanger, she hands it toward me.

Black as midnight with three quarter sleeves and a Queen Ann neckline, the dress has black buttons all the way down the front. The length is demure, with a hemline that ends right below my knees, but the front slit begins at mid-thigh and the silk fabric hugs my figure beautifully. The sexy dress shows off all my assets but doesn't make me look like I'm trying too hard. The Louboutin black fishnet heels with gold trim will be my only accessory.

Once dressed, I look in the mirror, pleased. Annie grins, throws up one eyebrow, and growls.

"Mm-hmm. Mystery man won't know what hit him."

I hope so, I think.

***

Winter 1772, Burgundy Region, France

I shake. The gooseflesh stands out on my arms like anthills. Any moment now, my father will walk through the door and hold out his arm for me. This is the last time I will sit at the mahogany vanity that was my mother's. Never again will I wake to the sun streaming from the floor length windows onto the familiar grey walls covered with hand painted gold leaves. In a few short hours, I will ride off in a gilded carriage, fit for a newly married Marchioness.

DEEPEST MIDNIGHT

Charles, the Marquis of Mirabeau is not who I want. I don't know who I would have wanted, given the chance, but it isn't him.

I wasn't even allowed to help with the design of my wedding gown, my husband did that. The dress is a fine robin's egg blue silk with white lace ruffles at the elbows and a jeweled bodice which sparkles with crystals and pearls. I wear diamond teardrop earrings, a pearl choker, and a floral diamond clasp holds the back of my pouffed hair perfectly in place. Face powdered, lips and cheeks rouged, I am ready to ascend the ranks of nobility.

The gown is stunning. But, I am nothing more than ornamentation. My vile, hated corset is cinched so tightly, I can scarce breathe. I typically wear the contraption as loose as possible, a tactic not allowed, today.

A soft knock on the door makes me want to cry. The back of my throat tightens, and my eyes burn. I hold the feeling back. I will keep my head high and not let my father see me crying. I straighten my back and let a cold veil of ice fall over my face.

"Come in, father," *I call out.*

I am shocked when the Dauphine, Marie Antoinette herself, swishes into the room. She is magnificent. Long plumes of white feathers spray from the top of her perfectly coiffured, powdered hair. Her golden, silk gown is draped in rows of gold organza ribbon, white bows, and pink rosettes, which set off the pink of her lips and cheeks perfectly. Her jewels, rope after rope of brilliant, iridescent pearls, click as she walks.

I immediately stand, dropping into a prim curtsy before my queen. Charles had boasted that the Dauphine would attend our wedding, but I had not believed him.

She places her tiny hand under my elbow. "Stand up, my dear, and let me look at you." *Her voice is sweet, but commanding. I stand, feeling awkward as I tower over her. Only a year older than I am, she possesses such poise and confidence.*

"Yes, your Royal Highness. We are honored by your presence today."

She giggles and sits on the bench at the foot of my bed, her gown almost swallowing her whole.

"So, formal. Call me Marie. I can see why Charles chose you. You are very lovely, you remind me of a swan with that long, elegant neck."

"Thank you," *I blush.*

"Come here and hold out your wrist. I'm going to give you your wedding gift."

I do as she bids, standing in front of her with my arm out. From the folds of her gown, she brings forth a glittering bracelet of large, square sapphires surrounded by intricate swirls of cut diamonds. For a moment, I am speechless. This gift is worth more than my father's entire estate.

"It's exquisite, and so generous." I know better than to offend her by protesting. *"Thank you, I shall always treasure it."*

"Please do, it's a treasure in itself!" Marie laughs, and I join her. *"Charles is a childhood friend of my husband. He has always been loyal. We shall all be good friends, and we hope to have you at court very soon."*

With that, she floats up, kisses me on both cheeks and sweeps out in a rustle of gold, ribbons, and pearls.

I can't help but smile after her, until my gaze falls on my father, standing aside and bowing for the Dauphine. My tall, relatively fit father still has copious amounts of dark hair. His hardness is his face. Deeply lined around his cold gray eyes and unsmiling mouth, he looks much older than his forty years. Father had an expensive suit of dark blue silk embroidered with gold brocade made for this momentous occasion. He must look the part—a man wealthier than he is. Father walks into the room and examines my wrist.

"Aren't you lucky to receive such a gift. Don't lose it." He puts out his arm for me to take. There is no compliment, no words of fatherly advice, and I don't expect any.

Father spared no expense on this grand affair. To all the world, it looks as if a loving man is seeing his only daughter off in style. I know better. Father loves to show off his wealth, what little he has left. Hundreds of his most superficial friends, descended on the chateau to heap their congratulations on a man whose vanity knows no end.

The wedding is lovely. Everywhere I look my gaze falls upon a smiling face. My own smile is frozen in place. I will play my own part, with all the grace I can muster.

CHAPTER FOUR

The doorbell startles me out of my reverie, causing me to jump about five feet. What an embarrassment to vampires everywhere. Sitting on the edge of my bed, taking deep breaths, I need to get a grip on myself. I stand to take one final look in the mirror. I can't remember the last time I was so worried about my appearance. The voices of Annie and Alexandre float up to me, as they greet our guests.

Opening the door, I walk slowly down the stairs, cross the hall, and into our white-paneled living room. This room, decorated by Alexandre, is slightly ostentatious with raised, embossed Venetian plaster designs lining the doorway and ceiling trim. It fits his personality to a tee.

"There you are Mills. I was beginning to wonder if we could expect you."

Leave it to Alexandre to bring the entire room's focus onto me. He takes my hand and begins introductions. First, of course, is Kathryn. She smiles, tilting her shoulder toward me in a way which makes me think she is trying to be seductive.

However, Alexandre's lust is well placed. She is striking with black hair cut short in a bob, green eyes that sparkle, a full pouty mouth, and creamy skin. She is tall in her very high heels, but not as tall as I am. Her figure is nice, and her wrap dress is chic in a classic bright yellow. Not a color everyone can pull off, but she does, beautifully.

Next, I shake hands with the director, James. He is a nondescript man I would describe as mousy, had he been female. He also keeps wiping his mouth, reminding me I need to wash my hands. Then comes Timothy Woods, the movie star. He is certainly handsome with dark, thick, wavy hair and beautiful dark brown eyes. He has a killer smile but is awfully short.

"Millicent, I love that name," says Timothy.

He bends to kiss my hand, trying to be charming, but misses the mark. His eyes travel all over my body, never making it to my face.

Finally, Alexandre steers me over to the only person in the room who I have any interest in knowing. I take a deep breath and look into his eyes. *I can do this.* Physically, this man is an exact copy of Julien. With my heels on, we are face to face.

Alexandre says, "Millicent Mirabeau, meet Jack Thomas."

The moment our hands meet, he says, "It's a pleasure to meet you Ms. Mirabeau. I believe I saw you last night on the riverfront."

The voice, oh my god, the voice. Before I know it, my knees have buckled, sending me teetering to the side. Jack and Alexandre both reach out to steady me. Annie runs over, slipping an arm around my waist.

"Too much damn humidity in the air today. Let's get some water," she says, pulling me out of the room.

Once out of sight in the kitchen, I lean against the counter and cover my face with my hands. I'm embarrassed, but I can't help but realize that not only did he see me last night, he remembered seeing me.

"How can two people have the same voice? His voice is what made me lose it. I can't believe what just happened. What kind of immortal gets weak in the knees? Great," I whine.

"You'll figure it out, but don't worry about the buckling. Before you came down, Kathryn was complaining about how she felt faint all afternoon from the extreme mugginess. We'll go with the same thing for you. Sip on this water for appearances. The best thing to do to save face is to go right back out again."

She is right. Annie lets me lead the way and in we go. When we return, everyone is seated. Walking in, the men all stand, except for Timothy, and inquire as to how I am. It's nice to know, for the most part, chivalry isn't dead.

Annie says, "She's fine just a little overheated from today. Never drinks enough water."

Kathryn chimes in with, "Today was just awful. I don't know how you stand it. Is it like this year-round?"

"It isn't always so bad. Most of the time, the weather is quite pleasant. I suppose you get used to it," I reply.

The men, who stood, resume their seats. Annie sits next to the cold fireplace, which we left unlit this evening for the comfort of our human guests. I take the only other empty spot, on the loveseat, next to the man I know as Julien. Alexandre looks at me and doesn't seem happy.

"Can I get you a drink, Mills, or are you good with water for now?" He asks, eyes narrowed.

"I'm fine, Alexandre, thank you," I answer, my voice clipped.

He turns his attention back to Kathryn and the director, who is sitting awfully close to her. I know this annoys Alexandre, who I'm sure, just wants to get her alone. Kathryn begins talking to the room about her character in the film, a dead woman who regenerates to take revenge on the men who killed her. Sounds pretty B-movie to me, but I keep that to myself.

Timothy, who is seated in a chair next to the loveseat, leans toward me with his eyes on my legs, and says, "This is a lovely home. Is it Alexandre who owns it? You're all roommates?"

This is one of the most difficult things about being around mortals and why most of our kind avoids them like the plague. They are nosy. It can be difficult to explain living situations without making them think you're weird or up to something.

Our money is separate and has grown tremendously, thanks to Alexandre's financial prowess. While, Alexandre had money before I came around, he's never been too open about where it came from. My money originated with the gold, jewels, and artwork taken from my mortal life and later sold.

I explain to Timothy that the house is mine, but it's a family home and Annie and Alexandre are my cousins. Timothy takes what I say at face value, adding he is also close with his family. He's blinking too much, making me think he's probably lying. I try to look somewhat interested but could care less about getting to know him. It is quite clear he's usually the center of the universe, it's also clear he is used to dominating conversations. His voice is loud, and his gigantic smile never wavers.

I throw a look over at Annie. She is clearly amused, but does her friendly duty, bringing her chair in closer to Timothy. In a sweet, sexy voice, Annie asks him to tell her more about the film they're working on. As Timothy is quite happy to continue talking, with his eyes firmly attached to Annie's chest, I turn my body slightly toward Jack. He has remained quiet, while sipping his drink, never speaking with anyone.

"So, Jack, is this your first time in Savannah?"

Lame, I know, but you have to start somewhere.

"Actually, yes. I've become quite taken with it, such a unique place."

I hear what I missed before, a slight English accent. Not French. He looks me right in the eyes as he tells me about all the things he has enjoyed in the last few days. Those eyes, the color of lapis, could hold my attention for an eternity. I wish everyone else in the room would disappear.

"How much longer will filming continue?" I ask.

"Six to eight more weeks. Although, you never really know. It could end up taking a little longer."

Plenty of time for me to figure this out. We fall into an easy conversation. He is a writer, as well as an actor. I also learn he is from London and has been acting for twenty years, almost always in character parts.

I apologize for my lack of film knowledge. He laughs. "Being a character actor, I tend to blend into a film anyway. You may have seen me many times and not noticed."

Not likely.

This feels very easy. Jack is far from the snob Alexandre accused him of. He is kind and genuinely interested in speaking with me. Not once have his eyes wandered from my face. He seems as intent on me, as I am on him.

I take a moment to look around the room and notice people look bored. I'm not terribly concerned with how the others are feeling, but this may be my opportunity to get Jack alone for a few minutes.

Taking a risk, I place my hand on Jack's arm. I suggest, as a writer, he may have an interest in seeing our library.

He leans in, conspiratorially, and says just loudly enough for me to hear, "I'd love to see it," in a way that sends shivers down my spine.

I wonder how I'm going to get him in there alone, the last thing I want is anyone to join us. Deftly, Annie suggests we take the party into the courtyard, as the evening has cooled off nicely. Everyone readily agrees.

Annie grabs two bottles, winks at me and leads the way. I look over at Jack, to see if he's noticed the wink, but he doesn't give any indication. While everyone is getting up, Jack and I purposely hold back, like two kids with a secret plan.

"Perfect timing. It's almost as if she knew what we were thinking," Jack says, as we find ourselves alone in the living room.

"Almost." If only he knew how right he is.

I show Jack across the hall to the library, easily the most perfect room in the house. We pause in front of the antique door. Imported from France, the gray finish door, with intricately carved wooden panels, looks like a gateway to another world. I chose it specifically for this room.

Opening the door, we step inside, Jack in front. He walks into the center of the room, hands in the pockets of his black pants, head turning every which way. I give him time. There is much to take in.

"A reader's dream; I could spend all day in here."

"Thank you that was my intention."

Antique, gray-washed built-ins with silver leafed scalloped edges line the walls. At the far end of the room, stands an aged, white, wrought iron, spiral staircase. The staircase leads to a second story of the same built-ins, all filled with books. Books are everywhere; in the cases, stacked on the floor, in piles on the desk, and several litter the end tables. There is a cushioned, silk couch, and two matching chairs in the center of the room, where hangs a large crystal chandelier.

"Alexandre says the room is too feminine for his liking."

"It's beautiful, just like the woman who designed it."

He seems embarrassed by his comment, as he turns away as quickly as he had turned to face me. I try not to smile like an idiot.

"Are you really interested in books to this extent?" he asks.

I should probably be offended, but I also wonder why he would ask this.

"I am. Why do you seem surprised?"

"Maybe I've just spent too much time on movie sets. In my experience, girls who look like you, are only interested in clothes, jewelry, and makeup."

"Wow, jaded much? I think maybe you are stereotyping pretty girls. How many of them have you actually tried getting to know?"

"Good point, that wasn't fair. You just surprised me, and people rarely surprise me, anymore. I hope I didn't offend you."

"Of course not. Would you like to go out and join the others?"

"Not really, can we sit in here for a while?"

"I'd like nothing more. I'm not sure I would call this a party, anyway. Would you?"

"I'm not really a party kind of guy, so this suits me just fine. I'm infinitely more comfortable around books than people."

"I know the feeling. Strange that you chose acting as a profession then."

"It truly was. More than anything acting was an escape for me, a way out of a small town for a young man with few options."

He pauses. After a moment, he sits on the couch, where he begins to tap his foot.

"There is something very familiar about you, but I know I would have remembered you, had we met before."

He knows me. I want to jump up and down like a child filled with excitement on Christmas morning. It's everything I can do to remain serene, because jumping up and down wouldn't seem strange, at all.

"Is there?" I ask, sitting next to him.

"Yes, when I saw you last night, I thought for a second that I knew you."

"Admittedly, I feel the same. Almost like Déjà vu."

He nods, his brow wrinkling, "Yeah, just like that. Funny."

He says funny almost like a side note, like he's trying to convince himself that it is easily explained. I know it isn't.

Jack is close to me now, I can feel the warmth from his breath and body. He has a slightly musky, sandalwood scent that makes me quiver. It seems his nature is to be a little timid, but physically he is all man. My desire roars to life. It's all I can do to not lean in and kiss him. It's easy to imagine us sitting in this room, a fire in the grate, my feet in his lap, reading lines from our favorite books to each other.

This is my moment, "You said how much you have enjoyed the jazz down here. The next night you're free, I would love to take you to a small, wonderful little out-of-the-way jazz place."

"We have a late filming schedule tomorrow, but I would love to, after. It may be late, around midnight." It's cute he thinks midnight is late for me.

"Midnight is when things pick up around here, that's perfect."

I can tell by the way his body is positioned and the way his eyes are locked onto mine that he feels the same way about the kissing, but something is holding him back. Societal mores, I hope.

"I promise tomorrow night will be a lot more fun than tonight has been." *Hopefully, in more ways than one.*

He laughs. "I've quite enjoyed this night."

I begin hearing Alexandre in my head; wondering what we're up too. Not long after, Jack and I rejoin the others to finish out the night.

Later, as we move out onto the porch to say goodbye to our guests, Kathryn pulls me aside. She also pulls me away from Jack. I try not to let the irritation show on my face.

"Um, Millicent? Can I talk to you in private for a sec?" she says, in a barely audible whisper.

"Sure, let's go back in the living room."

I already know she wants to ask me about Alexandre. I take her tiny handbag, tossing it behind the door.

"Hey guys, hang on. Kathryn left her bag inside." I close the door, pick up her purse, and we walk into the living room.

"Thanks, you're pretty quick. I can appreciate that," she says, her smile lovely.

"You have to be fast thinking around Alexandre. You never know what he's going to say, or do," I joke, hoping that gives her the transition she's looking for.

"Speaking of Alexandre…Is he seeing anyone, right now?"

"Nope. Are you interested in him?" I ask, wondering if she can see right through me.

"Well, yes. I mean look at him. He looks like he stepped off the *300* set."

I purse my lips, nodding my head. If only she knew, Alexandre is his own walking ego.

"He is definitely a perfect male specimen, physically."

"Just physically? Is he a jerk or something?"

"No, no. That isn't what I meant. Alexandre is great, he's my family. I wouldn't spend so much time with him if he was awful."

"That's what I wanted to hear. Thanks, Millicent. I wanted to be sure about what I'm possibly getting myself into."

"Getting into?"

She blushes, undetectably to the human eye. "He followed me to the restroom. Not in a creepy way. He was just looking for an opportunity to talk to me alone...nothing happened. He asked if I would like to come back later, after we all left. It was kind of cute. He almost seemed shy about asking."

Don't laugh, Millicent, don't laugh. "Uh-huh, that's Alexandre to a tee; shy and discreet. What did you say?"

"Oh, I'll be back. I've been dying to meet someone like him. Who knows what could happen?"

"Who knows," I echoed.

She was actually quite nice. I hoped Alexandre wouldn't break her heart. She was clearly looking for more, but she was right, who knows what would happen? They were both adults, free to make their own decisions.

CHAPTER FIVE

Last night, after our guests departed, Annie and I plopped ourselves on my bed to debrief. Kathryn returned. No shocker, there. They were currently occupied, and not quietly, I might add. Annie was all ears as I recounted my conversations with Jack. I wasn't any closer to figuring him out.

"Julien was soft spoken, but not shy. He would have made sure I understood what he wanted on that couch. Jack held himself back. I'm trying not to get my hopes up, but I should know a lot more after our date."

"So, is he Julien? Do you think it's a past life kind of thing?" Annie asks.

"Physically. However, Jack's personality is definitely unique. I need to do more research, but what we already discovered is that a soul can reincarnate and be completely different in the next life."

"Meaning he could have Julian's face, and even his soul, but be a completely different person," summarizes Annie.

"Yeah. He seems pretty cool, but what if he turns out to be awful? It will be hard for me to turn away from him, looking the way he does. All I need is another horrid man in my life. You know all about Charles, but there was also my father."

I tell Annie how my father skulked around the chateau for three years, after bringing home his new wife. It was a dark, miserable time. Father's goal was to conceive a legitimate heir for his diminishing fortune and title. I'm sure he believed his young bride would bear him many children, mostly sons. His second wife became more of a failure, in his eyes, than the first had been. He made sure she knew how he felt. Poor Sabina could not have a live child, try as she might. There were several pregnancies, all of which either ended in miscarriage or stillbirth.

It was awful for her. I could see her deteriorate with each fresh, horrible tragedy. Father was completely unsympathetic. Of course, there were illegitimate children of father's out in the world and at least two boys I heard whispers of. What he needed was a non-bastard. I, as a girl, was useless to him.

Sabina was always indifferent to me, neither cruel nor kind. She had been ill-used by my father. She only wanted to love and be loved in return. The poor girl did not deserve her fate. She died when I was fifteen, a young woman of twenty-five, whose body could take no more.

"That is one terrible story, Mills. No wonder you jumped at the chance to be with Julien. After being raised by a hard man like your father, and then being married to another hard, cold man like Charles, who wouldn't?"

"You've got that right. Hopefully, the future will be a little brighter."

I wake the next evening to find Annie gone. She is like a cat, always sneaking in and out and on the prowl. After feeding last night, I won't need blood for another week or so, but I have several hours to fill and need to keep myself occupied. I decide to amuse myself with some late-night shopping.

There is a boutique nearby which I love, but the owner Tess, closes at six. On occasion, she will re-open for me. Particularly, since I tend to spend large amounts of cash in a short amount of time, making me an ideal customer. I send Tess a text, lying in bed until I receive a reply. Five minutes later, Tess answers saying she will meet me at her shop in thirty minutes. Throwing on my usual skinny jeans and loose tee, I'm out the door.

The streets are alive as always. I feel a hopeful lightness. A girl could get used to this. Approaching the door of the boutique, I hear a soft click and the door opens, letting a flood of light onto the sidewalk. There is Tess, a lovely full-figured lady, wearing sweatpants, printed with cats.

"I was about to put in a movie when you texted," she says, by way of explanation.

"Sorry Tess. I have a date tonight, for the first time in a hundred years, and wanted something new."

She has no idea how serious I am about the hundred years' thing.

"Always happy to open for you, Millicent. The new stock is in the front of the store."

Not known for her wordiness, Tess leaves me, going to the back room. She knows I love looking through the racks alone, and don't need any help finding treasure. After only a few minutes, I spot a gold sequined skirt which is a must. I pick out my size along with a black, sleeveless, silk top to go with it. Then, I snatch up a pair of mid-heel, black, Jimmy Choo pumps. I grab a few other things that catch my eye, wanting to make it worth Tess's time. As she checks me out, she oohs and aahs over my choices, then thanks me for my patronage. I'm pretty sure Annie and I alone help keep the doors to this little place open.

Back at home, I bathe, starting to get ready. Effortless is the word of the day. Unlike when I was mortal, and everything was over the top and frothily decadent. Even as a child, I was powdered, coiffured, and costumed. A trend during my later years as a mortal had women decorating their hair with crazy, ostentatious flair. I wasn't a fan, but the ladies in my circle regularly added pastel colored wigs to their natural hair. They would often try to outdo each other with bolder, more elaborate creations, adding everything from butterflies to miniature sailing ships to the top of their already towering hairstyles. I admit, it was fun to see what the bolder ladies would do next.

I always preferred subtle, leaving my long hair loose and my makeup light. I add a simple gold bracelet, my favorite black leather clutch, and I'm ready. Alexandre walks in.

"You look beautiful," he says.

"You're being nice. You must have had fun last night," I tease.

"It was ok," he pauses a moment. "Lackluster, actually, though I'll give her points for enthusiasm."

"Poor Alexandre. You haven't had much luck in that department lately. Will you see her again?"

"It is fun bedding a movie star, maybe I can teach her a thing or two. Look, Mills, I came in to talk to you about this Jack."

Here we go.

"Go for it."

"Please tread carefully. Something about this doesn't feel right to me. I would like to avoid another blood bath. It would be a shame if we had to leave the city, unable to return for a hundred years."

The blood bath comment is referring to the revenge he took on my long-ago husband. I recall the front steps of my husband's chateau dripping with blood, the gravel of the round drive soaked with liquid that shone like black pools in the starlight. I had to hold up my gown, trying not to slip in the sticky mess. I am not taking this lightly, I also know Alexandre is deadly serious. However, being that I'm finally in a good mood, and in a hurry, I try to keep this brief, and light.

"Don't be so dramatic, Alexandre. Everything will be fine. I've no husband this time to ruin my life." I smile at him, receiving nothing in return but a smirk.

"Just watch your back, please. You've been a good companion to me."

"Aww. That was actually sentimental." I wink, blowing a kiss toward Alexandre at the same time.

"I'm serious, Mills."

"Ok, I get it. I will keep my eyes open, promise." I cross my fingers over my heart.

Alexandre walks me down the stairs. Trying to still my shaky limbs, I excitedly head toward the club. Not surprisingly, the speakeasy, is already packed at eleven-forty-five. Luckily, I called ahead and reserved my favorite dimly lit, corner booth. I order a martini, then sit back to wait for Jack. I have a laugh at a modern establishment, which is in no way secret or illegal, calling itself a speakeasy.

Jack walks in about ten minutes later wearing all black, once again. I'm completely fine with this, as he looks delectable. His black shirt is open at the collar, tucked into nicely fitted black slacks with expensive, tasteful, Ferragamo black loafers. The open shirt collar reveals a peak at a nicely toned chest. In his hand he holds a paperback.

Looking around the room, he smiles when he spots me. Scooting in so we are less than an arm's length away from each other, he surprises me by leaning in the rest of the way and kissing me on the cheek. A good start, but we can do better. I'm aching everywhere for the touch of this man but that's no reason to throw myself at him.

"You look stunning, Millicent." The scent of sandalwood fills my head with erotic thoughts. "I brought you a little something. My favorite book. It's my copy, so it's a little beat up."

His deep blue eyes are intent on mine, and again I have a hard time keeping my hands to myself. I wonder if his gaze is this intense for everyone. The thought makes me fiercely jealous. I want these eyes all to myself. All he has to do is look my way and I feel my breath quicken. This is what I want, something just like this. I had it once and was almost destroyed when I lost it.

I turn the book around in my hands. It's a copy of *The Moveable Feast* by Earnest Hemingway. I read it years ago but won't tell Jack this. "I love a dog-eared paperback, and I haven't read this. Thank you." I place the book in my lap. "You look nice, yourself. How was filming?"

Before he can answer, the waiter comes over to get his drink order. He orders a beer, then turns his attention back to me.

"It went well. We had some trouble with noise from the onlookers, but nothing that we couldn't work around. The crowd was trying to get a glimpse of Kathryn and Timothy."

I smile and shake my head. The interest in celebrities never changes, not from one century to the next. I remember the clamor over Marie Antoinette at my wedding, not to mention my own excitement at meeting her. Escapism from drudgery is what we all seek, this is what our pop culture icons represent.

We continue the usual get to know you banter from last night. I fudge some of my answers, out of necessity. If I said I was a two-hundred-forty-year-old vampire and minor French royalty, he would run as fast as he possibly could, thinking me utterly insane. Not a good way to start a first date.

Jack seems to have had a pretty normal life. He was born and raised in London by good, middle-class parents. An only child, he started acting in high school, is now thirty-eight and able to support himself with his profession. I'm not getting anything the least bit off about him, other than that he is not making a move on me. I notice he is tapping his foot again, which makes me grin. I guess I'll be making the first move.

"This place is great. I'm glad to be alone with you," says Jack.

I think this is an incredibly sweet thing to say, but playfully remind him, "We were alone last night, in the library."

"That doesn't count, not with everyone else in the courtyard wondering what we were up to."

"We weren't up to anything. It was all perfectly innocent, unfortunately." I wink at him, deciding it's time to get serious. I'm trembling, even though he hasn't touched me yet.

"Jack, I'm going to be blunt with you. A woman should never give up the higher ground, however, I feel like with you being in town for only a short while, our time is limited. I find you incredibly attractive. Are you at all interested in me?"

He laughs, "I appreciate a woman who doesn't play games, Millicent. You are truly a gorgeous woman. I'd be crazy not to be interested in you. To be honest, I'm just a little worried about the age difference. I'm quite a bit older than you."

I forget sometimes that my outside appearance froze at twenty-four, while internally, I have continued to grow and age. It also strikes me that if he is concerned about our age difference, he must see me as more than just an on-location fling. Only a gentleman would be concerned by my age, rather than running out the door to hail a cab.

"Believe me, Jack, I'm very mature for my years. And I'm just interested in getting to know you better and having fun. I'm not looking for anything serious, at the moment."

Jack grins, nodding his head. He looks down for a moment as if considering what to say next. He takes a breath and looks in my eyes. I drop my chin and shoulder, so that I'm looking slightly upward at him. This is the moment I've been waiting for. Apparently, my body language has the desired effect.

Jack lowers his gaze to my mouth and cups the back of my head in his hand. He pulls me toward him. When our lips meet, I take in a breath, ever so slightly, opening my mouth to his. The instant his tongue slides over mine, my skin heats up. It's a familiar sensation, which has long been dormant. My left-hand slides over his chest and I pull at his shirt, bringing our bodies closer. Inhaling his clean, masculine scent, my cheek brushes against his light five o'clock shadow.

I forgot the heart pounding excitement of the first kiss. Only one other time have I ever felt this intense desire, from one encounter. This kiss is familiar, yet new, at the same time. Jack deepens the kiss, and I want to lose myself in this moment. The dark, corner booth was a good choice.

Time feels as if it has stopped. All the waiting, all the loneliness, has been worth it for this one moment. If only I could go back to tell myself to be patient, that he would find me, again. I could go on kissing him like this, forever, but I need more.

After a couple of minutes of bliss, I break the kiss. "Time to go."

Clearly, we're on the same page. Pulling out his wallet, without a word, Jack leaves a fifty-dollar bill on the table. We hold hands, our bodies pressed against each other as we walk outside. Giddiness, once again, makes me feel jittery. It's been a long time since I felt such anticipation. Once outside, Jack hooks his arm around my waist, then pulls me in for another kiss. Against my mouth, he asks me where I would like to go.

"Wherever you're staying."

We hail a cab and are off.

CLARA WINTER

CHAPTER SIX

The only part of the hotel room that interests me is the king-size bed. Entering the living space, I set my clutch and Jack's book on the coffee table and slip out of my shoes at the same moment. Why waste time? Jack steps up behind me and pushes my hair aside. He brings his other hand around my waist, resting it on my stomach. I feel his breath as he dips his head to kiss the space between my shoulder and neck. Leaning back against him, he slowly kisses his way to my ear.

This man is heaven. I feel as if I could fall in love with him in an instant. I have missed this feeling, even more so than I realized. His right-hand dips into my blouse and he gently massages my breast over my bra for a moment, before his fingers push inside of the lacey material and cup my bare breast. I can't help but moan. Wanting more, I turn toward him. My mouth is greedy on his as I unbutton his shirt, peel it off and throw it on the floor. I step back, and he pulls my blouse over my head. I unhook my bra, letting the undergarment fall on the growing pile of clothes.

We are completely in sync with each other. There's no awkwardness. It's as if we've done this a hundred times, but the excitement is still fresh. With his hands at the small of my back, he bends down to kiss and suck my breasts. Letting my head fall back, I close my eyes. *Good call on the skirt with the elastic waist.* It is easily pulled down along with my panties and kicked aside.

Everything about Jack is extraordinary. He takes me to the bed, stopping to grab a condom out of his suitcase. We take our time, savoring every inch of each other. Jack brings me right to the brink of pleasure with his expert tongue and hands.

Ready to feel him inside me, I push him onto his back. He enters me as I straddle him, sitting up to kiss me while I begin to ride. He holds on to my backside, guiding me up and down. There is no hurry, only a desire to feel him. I think of how I would love to be locked with him, like this, forever. It's been a long time since I felt anything for any man, and I luxuriate in this. I don't let myself hope for too much, but it's hard when I feel as if I am coming back to life, after two centuries.

Feeling my climax, I quicken my movements until I cry out. Jack grips me tighter, bringing me down, again and again, until he climaxes. He collapses backward, pulling me down on top of him, and we lay panting on the bed. He continues to hold me tightly as I lay with my head on his chest. Feeling like life has returned, I listen to his heart beating, his breath exhaling rapidly on the top of my head.

"I won't be cliché and say that was amazing," he says into my hair.

"Neither will I."

An hour later, I'm reluctantly dressing to leave.

"You can stay," he says from the bed.

I lean down to kiss him long and slow. He tries to pull me back into bed, but I pull back.

"I have some things to do early in the morning."

He looks skeptical but doesn't say anything.

"Maybe we can do this again tonight," I offer.

"We better do this again, as soon as possible."

"Text me when you're free." I blow him a kiss, as I leave the room.

Smiling and feeling blissful, I lean against the wall of the elevator, pressing my fingers to my lips. I feel just as I did over two hundred years ago, after being with Julien for the first time. I try to remind myself Jack clearly isn't Julien, not as I knew him. But, whatever this is and whoever he is, I'll take it.

Once home, I shut the door behind me with only twenty minutes to spare before sunrise. Slipping off my shoes at the threshold, I walk into the living room. Alexandre has an open book in his hands, while Annie plays with her phone. Annie looks up and her eyes narrow, "Well, well, well. It looks as if the cat got the mouse."

"Maybe," I say, throwing her a wink.

Alexandre glances at me over his book.

"Don't worry, Alexandre. Everything is fine. Better than fine."

I turn and bounce up the stairs. I'm too exhausted to change, so I peel off my clothes before diving between the silky sheets. Just as I'm about to drift into nothingness, my door opens.

Alexandre sits on the edge of my bed, looking down at me, in a way that is familiar. He hasn't looked at me that way in at least one hundred fifty years, it gives me the bad kind of shivers. I pull the blankets up higher.

"What? I'm tired."

"I've missed you, that's all. Maybe I could sleep in here tonight?"

"Are you joking? We haven't shared a bed in well over a century."

"Don't get excited, I just want to sleep in here, so we can talk. I'll be a good boy."

I'm almost dumbfounded, I forget how to speak. Alexandre must take my silence as an invitation because he gets up to move to the other side of the bed. I find my voice damn quick.

"Alexandre, not tonight. If you want to talk, I would love to do only that, tomorrow. It's freaky for you to sleep in here. You know I've just slept with another man."

Alexandre looks at me with a cold, unsmiling face. "As you wish. You have to know that I can't allow this, Mills. You had your fun tonight, but this needs to be the end of it," he says as he moves toward the door.

I think he must be joking and laugh. "It's almost dawn, my dear maker. Can we be funny tomorrow?"

"I'm deadly serious, Mills. This is going to end up being more than just play, I can see it in your face. I forbid you from seeing him again. There are details you don't know about our ways. I have kept you safe, naïve all these years. Therefore, I'm telling you as your master, to end it."

My mouth drops open, but before I can respond, Alexandre leaves the room. He has never called himself my master before, and I don't like it one bit. What this tells me is Alexandre thinks of me as his property. He should know me well enough, to know this would be something which would upset me, having been considered property by my husband and my father. His sudden coldness reminds me of my father and how fearful he made me feel as a child. But, before I can think two more thoughts, I'm out.

***

Summer 1763, Burgundy Region, France
Trying to still my breathing is difficult with the fragrant blooms of lavender all around me. I want to bury my face in the buds and inhale deep gulps of scented air. If I do that, I'll be found out and lose the game.

"There you are!" exclaims Blanche.

Laughing, she runs toward me, black hair swinging loosely behind her, dark brown eyes shining with motherly love. The only motherly love, I've ever known.

"How did you find me?" I giggle.

"It was hard. You're becoming better at hiding, all the time."

She scoops me up into her strong arms. My arms and legs, long for my age, wrap around her. If only I could always feel safe and warm, like this. Having just turned seven, I am already quite tall. I know she will not be carrying me much longer.

Blanche sets me on my feet, taking my small, delicate hand in her strong and steady one. We turn toward the chateau, walking side by side.

"I fear father will be home soon."

"Hush, child. There is nothing to fear."

I know this isn't exactly true. Everyone at the chateau finds my father scary. He was grumpy and mean. Several times, I saw him put good people on the street for the slightest offense. When I knelt for my evening prayers, I always asked God to watch over Blanche, the closest person I've ever had to a real parent.

"What will we read today?" I asked, hoping for another delightful story.

"Today, we will work on your writing. We have been neglecting schoolwork. Your penmanship is atrocious. My lord is adamant you possess the learning of a noblewoman."

I moan, kicking at the grass under my feet. I hate writing endless lines of the alphabet. A protest begins to form on my lips, when the very clear sound of wheels crunching over gravel reaches my ears.

My body tenses and my eyes look up at Blanche. Her warm, loving face has changed. It is now hard, cold, but I know it is not a look for me, but for who may be arriving. She drops my hand. Bending down in front of me, she quickly straightens my dress and pulls lavender buds from my hair.

Father is seldom around. His absences are the only time I am truly happy. Blanche allows me such freedom. There is running, playing, and laughing. It seemed as if nothing joyful was ever allowed when father was home.

We haven't seen him for two years. I try to remember what he looked like, but I can't picture him clearly. I only know how I feel. A shiver moves through me, even though I stand in the hot, summer sun. Why can't he just stay away forever?

Blanche and I walk to the front of the house, then stand like statues by the main door, waiting for the carriage to pull up. I feel sick but do my best to imitate Blanche. Standing with your back perfectly straight is hard, and my knees shake.

"Be still, Millicent," Blanche whispers.

We wait, in silence, as the footman places the block in front of the carriage door. Father doesn't wait for the footman but opens the door himself and steps out. He squints his gray eyes in the bright sunlight, causing his entire face to crease. Turning back to the carriage, he offers his hand to a woman, now stepping out onto the block.

She is tiny and very young. Her light brown hair catches the light, making it look red for a moment. I can't help but think her big, round, dark eyes remind me of a doe. The kind I've seen many times galloping around the edges of the lawn. I can't explain it, but I want to tell her to run, to stay in the carriage and go home. Wherever that is.

The woman takes father's arm and they walk the short distance up the stairs to where Blanche and I wait.

"Millicent, this is your new mother, Sabina. I shall finally have an heir."

Being an unwanted girl, I have heard father say this before. I curtsy to this young lady, almost the same size as myself. Sabina regards me coldly, then turns to walk into her grand, new home. And the day had started so well.

Three years later, father caught us in the schoolroom, laughing and dancing. He dismissed my beloved Blanche on the spot. I never saw her again.

CLARA WINTER

CHAPTER SEVEN

The next evening, Alexandre is gone. He slipped a note under my door just to reiterate what he already told me.

"Mills, we've been together a long time and I've never asked you for much. End whatever it is you have with Jack. I foresee disaster if you don't. I am your master, don't force my hand. Just take care of it. I will be out of town for a few days, this will give you the time you need. I'm not a monster. With love, Alexandre."

I'm stunned, how can I not be? The three of us have had numerous trysts, sometimes with each other. Why does he care now? Alexandre has never been clear about a great many things. I should have pressed him for more answers earlier in my immortality. Annie is nowhere to be found, so I shrug my shoulders, muttering what Alexandre can go do with himself. He may be my maker, but he is certainly not my master. If he thinks I am going to give up my chance with Jack, he can think again.

It's hard to shake the weirdness of last night. After living together all this time, I can't convince myself Alexandre wanted me, physically. Likely, it was as he said, he only wanted company. I have been his constant companion, after all. His feelings were hurt when I asked him to leave, then he lashed out, pure and simple.

After living peacefully with him for two hundred forty years, I can't imagine it was anything more. Alexandre could be experiencing some sort of existential crisis, as all immortals do at some point. Instead of comforting him, I kicked him out. At this thought, I feel a little guilty. Alexandre has listened to me whine, complaining for centuries. Last night, all he received for his constant friendship was rejection

I'm about to reach out my mind and ask Alexandre for forgiveness when there is a sharp knock at the front door. More like a banging as if someone is hitting it with a battering ram. What in the world? Slipping on a robe, I dash down the stairs, throwing open the door.

James, the director of Jack's film, stands half hunched over on the porch. He straightens a bit to look at me. He looks like he hasn't shaved since I saw him at the cocktail party. His eyes are bloodshot, his hands are clenched into fists at his sides.

"James, can I help you?"

"Are they here?"

"I'm alone, is something wrong?"

"Kathryn left the set early, said she couldn't film tonight's scenes, because she had a headache. I followed her, then saw her get in a car with your friend."

I have no idea what to say, and furthermore, have no interest in getting involved. This isn't the first time Alexandre has found his way into the bed of an attached woman. But, I do find it odd Alexandre hasn't left town. He lied to me, but there is too much going on for me to care about what he is up to with Kathryn. I'm sure, I can guess.

"Look, James, all I can tell you is they're not here. If I see Kathryn, I'll let her know you are looking for her."

I begin to shut the door, when James slams it hard with his hand, keeping it open. His eyes have gone from bloodshot to crazy in the span of two seconds, which startles me a little.

"A better idea would be to tell Alexandre to leave her the hell alone."

He whirls around, practically jumping off the front steps.

Events couldn't get any more bizarre. After so many years of boredom, I'm not relishing this chaos. It reminds me of my past. Once I met Julien, my life spun quickly out of control. One minute I was married to a man I couldn't stand, the next I was madly in love, and the minute after finding the love of my life, I had lost everything. I should probably listen to the fear growing inside me, but I have a date with Jack. These crazy people can all have each other.

At least everyone's gone for now, so I can focus on other things. Jack and I have plans to meet back at his hotel. He wanted to meet for dinner, but I can't eat. What's the point of going through the motions of a date, when all we end up doing is tearing each other's clothes off, anyway? I said to eat without me, and I would see him after.

James has taken up my precious bath time, so I adjust, taking a quick shower instead. I choose a black cotton summer dress, with dark green strappy sandals. I'm used to long stretches of boring, so the events of the past days are making my head spin. The best remedy for a spinning head is to spend another night tangled in Jack's arms.

We do just that. I purposely leave out everything that happened with Alexandre, and James. No need to create any more confusion, there is enough of that going on, and Jack still doesn't know what I am. Something else that is on my mind.

Sliding out of the hotel bed, I pull my dress on over my head, as I am again getting ready to do my disappearing act.

"Ducking out again. Why don't you stay tonight?"

"I'm sorry. I feel like such a guy, but I have early morning obligations."

"You keep saying, obligations, but you never explain what the word means." He is prodding, as gently as he can.

"I'm involved with different charities around town. That's what rich girls do with their days." My attempt at a lame joke, but really just a pathetic excuse.

I need to come up with an actual cover if I'm going to keep this up. It would be so much easier to say, "I'm a vampire and need to get my beauty sleep between dawn and dusk."

Taking my leave, I head home. Once there, I get a call from Jack on my cell.

"You bolted out of here like the building was on fire."

I laugh, "Very funny. I'm sorry for rushing out, forgive me?"

"Of course. On the condition you spend the day with me tomorrow. *The actual day*. I was a little focused on other things tonight and forgot to tell you I have the day off. It occurs to me I've never seen you in the daylight."

In my mind, I picture a pile of ashes next to designer heels, as the sun shines brightly overhead. Worrying about what I look like in the daytime takes on a whole new meaning.

"I would love to but let me check my schedule and get back to you. Get some sleep and I'll call you later. Ok?"

"Do I have a choice?" he responds, a little sulkily.

"We all have choices. By the way, good choices in the bedroom last night."

I hope my humor will get me off the phone, buying me some time to think. The lightness I have been feeling dissipates a little.

With too many details at once, my head feels like it's swimming. Would turning Jack be a possibility? I've never done it before. I know the mechanics and it doesn't seem too hard, except for the possibility of his being unable to cope with the change. Would he even want to be what I am? Had Julien lived, I would never have wanted this. I wanted to live my life with Julien, have his children, and grow old with him. I know Jack has plans for his future. He told me about his next picture, which will finally see him as a leading man, something he has been working toward for a long time. As an actor with a familiar face, it may be difficult for him to disappear. A very important aspect to consider.

I put these thoughts aside and focus on what should be first. Is what we have more to Jack than just a fling? It feels like it. He is sweet and tender, always wanting me to stay. But, if he just sees me as a nice little on-location piece, everything else is moot. If I find out that he feels the same way I do, then I need to start worrying. And what about Alexandre? Do I now have to worry about what he'll do, on top of everything else? I can't imagine he's serious, but he has managed to thoroughly piss me off. He's always been on my side; I feel off without him to advise me.

I crawl between my sheets, burying my head under the mound of pillows. My bed has always been a sanctuary for me. Someplace I feel safe, comfortable. It's typical for a vampire to immediately fall into a death like sleep, but I have too much going on in my mind. I keep thinking about Julien, comparing him to Jack. If Jack didn't look exactly like Julien, I wouldn't have ever given him the time of day. That isn't fair to Jack, he is his own man and a pretty great one.

There's no denying the difference in personality. Julien knew he was attractive to women. Before meeting me, he used to bed women, left and right. He was anything but shy. Jack on the other hand, could certainly be defined as such. Had I not taken the lead, I'm not sure he'd have ever made a move. Jack seems unsure of himself, at times. In one of our bedroom conversations, he confessed he was genuinely surprised with his film success. He does not understand his appeal. Julien was confident in his work and himself, to the point of cockiness, but he was incredibly kind, as is Jack. Both men share creative abilities, along with bedroom prowess. However, I'm not convinced there are more differences, than similarities.

I tell myself to shut up and go to sleep. I don't think anything has ever been solved by worrying through the night, or in my case, through the day.

CLARA WINTER

CHAPTER EIGHT

I awake with an hour to go until dusk. Looking at my phone, I see Jack has left me a voicemail. A good indicator of his interest level.

"Hey night owl, not sure what time we will be wrapping up tonight. Could be a late one. Call me when you finish your *obligations* for the day, so we can coordinate."

I set down the phone and plant my feet on the ground. Opening the door to my bedroom, I walk through the dark hallway and descend the stairs. The lamps in the living room are on. I'm not the only one up early. Walking in, I see Annie reclining on the velvet sofa, pillows propped up behind her reading a book. Vampires do love a good book.

"What are you reading so early?" I ask my friend.

"A yummy romance. Look at this hot guy on the cover."

She holds the book cover toward me.

"Definitely hot, and a fireman, bonus."

Sitting down, I pull her feet onto my lap.

"I feel like I haven't seen you for weeks," Annie says. "Things must be going well with Julien... I mean Jack." She smiles and raises her signature eyebrow.

"Funny, and yes. Things are going well in *that* department. What have you been getting into lately?"

"Unfortunately, not much. I've been bored, and you should feel terribly guilty about it. I'm thinking of taking off for New

York, for a bit. With both you and Alexandre occupied, I guess I'm due for a change of scenery."

"A change of scenery sounds like a great idea. And as far as feeling guilty, apparently, you've forgotten the four years you spent with a certain German vampire, whose name I could never pronounce. You were practically tied to the man's hip, or some other appendage." We both giggle.

"What can I say, I have a soft spot for German guys. Alright, we are both guilty of putting sex above our friendship, on occasion. I forgive you."

"We have so much to talk about, I don't even know where to begin," I start.

Before I can get any further, Annie says, "You know it isn't possible to have a long-term relationship with a mortal, not without revealing what you are. A couple of weeks is one thing, much longer and they can't help but get suspicious."

She pauses, adding, "And let's call the situation what it is, Mills. You think this man is Julien and based on an unproven fact, you've fallen in love with him. Not hard to do, when you never stopped loving Julien in the first place."

I feel annoyed, begin to contradict her, but stop. I have fallen in love with Jack, rapidly. Another similarity between the two men. I fell for Julien in the course of three, incredible days. However, I know Jack isn't Julien. At least that's what I keep telling myself. It's hard not to see my old love, when Jack is his spitting image. It's all a little confusing.

"What would you do?" I ask with my head down, picking at her sock.

"You know what I'm going to say. Break it off. It's going to get very messy, if you don't." She considers something, "Knowing you the way I do, I'm sure you won't, you can't. In that case, you should reveal yourself in a way that is somewhat dramatic. He'll never believe you, unless you show him something he can't deny."

We sit for a few moments in silence. She's right. I want Jack in my life. The only way to do it, will be to tell him everything. Having never revealed myself before, I have no idea how to go about it. Personally, I've only ever known a few vampires, and I don't know any who have unveiled themselves to a human.

There are no rules against it that I know of. But, according to Alexandre, there's a lot I don't know. I have to wonder why he has kept me in the dark all this time. I have been far too complacent.

After several moments deep in thought, Annie says, "You could cut yourself and force him to watch it heal. Of course, this will likely traumatize him to no end, which could be amusing. You should also brace yourself for the fact he may not accept you. This isn't a life for everyone."

"Amusing for you, this is far from funny for me," I say, "This is all very sound advice and I appreciate it, but there is also something else going on."

I relate to her what happened with Alexandre, show her the note, and then tell her about James.

"Whoa. Let's start with Alexandre. Do you think this is a vampire thing, or a love thing?"

"Love thing? As in, Alexandre is in love with me? Don't be ridiculous. It's a vampire thing. A male, alpha vampire thing."

She doesn't look so convinced. "I wouldn't be so sure of that. Alexandre has kept you close to him and he's never left you alone for more than a few days at a time. I've observed him before when you've described a hook up. He doesn't like it, but for some reason has always kept it to himself. Jack is clearly more than a hookup."

"Alexandre is protective, and always has been. It's part of our history. You know how he visited me in my dreams as a mortal. If he wanted more, he would tell me. I don't know if you've noticed, but he isn't exactly a wallflower. Besides, he's with Kathryn, at the moment. Not exactly the behavior of a man in love with someone else. They must be holed up somewhere in the city, right now," I reason.

"Nope. She came banging on the door late last night, drunk and looking for him. It was just another fling for him, as they all are. She seems to be taking it hard, though. I felt bad for her. I even invited her in, but she refused."

"I'm not surprised. Alexandre could never be serious about anyone for very long, not even me. Don't forget that we were together, and he never batted so much as an eyelash when I ended it," I reply. "I suppose James will be happy to have his star back."

"Whatever you say, my friend. I love you, but you've never been able to see Alexandre very clearly."

Annie goes back to her book, as I wander upstairs. There is no need to continue the conversation. Annie can think what she likes. I know she is wrong. I call Jack, leaving a voicemail letting him know I am free anytime, and to call me when he's off for the night. I decide to soak my tension away in a hot, steaming bubble bath.

Stripping off my clothes, I turn on the tap. A bubble bath is one of my all-time favorite ways to relax. I sink into the bubbles, as the tub fills. Just as I turn off the flow of water, the doorbell rings. Please tell me that isn't Jack, here already. It's not quite dark yet, which means Annie can't open the door. I hear light footsteps, then Annie pokes her head into the bathroom.

"Your man is at the door, and it's still light out," she whispers, even though there would be no way for him to hear us.

"Damn." I get out, grabbing a towel. "How long until the sun is down?"

"About twenty minutes."

I jog into the bedroom and grab my phone, hitting Jack's number. He answers right away. "Shouldn't you be filming?" I ask, a little more abruptly than I mean too.

"Millicent, the most terrible thing has happened."

I can hear from his cracked voice, it's bad, and my stomach drops. I'm completely thrown off with no idea what to say.

"Kathryn was murdered. Her body was found in Bonaventure Cemetery this afternoon."

I'm stunned into silence. I think of the black-haired beauty, whose green eyes sparkled with life.

"Millicent?" Jack brings me back, "Can you let me in? I'm standing outside and feel a bit awkward."

"I'm not home," I stammer, trying to think fast, "had to run out. Can we meet somewhere? God, Jack, I'm so sorry."

"I'll just wait for you here. I don't want to be around anyone, but you, right now."

With my preternatural ears, I hear him sit down in the wicker rocking chair.

"Of course, that was stupid of me. I shouldn't be too long, I'm on my way back, now."

We hang up. I can't help but be touched that he wants to be with me, when he is clearly grieved, and in pain.

Kathryn's death makes me think of Jack. More specifically, how vulnerable he is. How vulnerable Julien was. It takes almost nothing to end a human life. If Jack wants zero to do with immortality, how can I possibly watch him become frailer as time passes? I have a sense of history repeating itself; love affairs, murder, and death. All I ever wanted was a simple life, a simple love. This is anything but simple.

CLARA WINTER

CHAPTER NINE

For the millionth time in my life, I pull on jeans, then grab a blousy, red t-shirt. While pulling my hair into a ponytail, I slip my feet into black ballet flats. Nervousness and shock, are not things I've experienced much as a vampire. Vampires are pretty much invulnerable, so there isn't a whole lot to be scared of.

There are only three ways a vampire can meet their end. The first and probably the most obvious danger, is the sun. It isn't instantaneous, but will do the job, given enough exposure. Then comes beheading and, lastly, immolation. The stake through the heart myth is just that, a myth. Our hearts don't beat, so what would be the point? I shouldn't be worried one bit, but that's a lie. What scares me now isn't my own end. I'm worried for Jack, and I'm worried about the course of our relationship.

Kathryn's death hits a little too close to home, putting us, especially Alexandre in the spotlight. He will likely be on the list of suspects, having just been involved with her. I can't imagine the list to be a long one. She was a nice person.

Annie left me, almost immediately, disappearing into her room. Her plan is to leave the house as soon as the sun sets, as she wants nothing to do with this. She may be my best friend, but we all have our limits. Sitting rigidly on the edge of my bed, I wait. The sound of Jack outside, pacing the length of the porch, increases my anxiety. Obviously, he is not all about sitting or smelling the flowers. He is tense, and I can feel it like a heaviness hanging in the air.

I look at the clock. It's time. Soundlessly, I glide through the house, out the back door. The courtyard is beautiful at dusk. Bathed in shadows it is otherworldly. As always, the scent of magnolia mixed with gardenias permeates the air. I take a moment, allowing the sound of the fountain, the soft rustling of leaves and tree branches to sooth my senses.

I launch myself quietly onto the roof of the house behind us and look out onto the street. It's quiet. A giant magnolia tree hides me as I touch down on the sidewalk. I'm not too worried about being seen, though. Mortals tend to see what they want and avoid thinking too much on anything incongruous with their version of reality. Or maybe, I just don't care tonight.

As I walk around the block, I practice deep breathing to steady my nerves. Of course, breathing exercises don't help in the least. My lungs don't actually absorb oxygen. If only there was such a thing as vampire yoga. What would that look like I wonder? I picture Alexandre contorting his body to get a better look at the ladies in downward facing dog.

A few minutes later, I'm approaching the front of my house. Jack is still pacing and hasn't seen me yet. Taking advantage, I pause to watch him a moment. I love this man. Not the man he reminds me of, but this man. I love his shyness, his tenderness. I love the way he looks at me, making me feel I am the only person in the world.

My feet start moving. Once I start up the front walkway, Jack stops pacing, moving to the middle of the porch to face me. His face is grim, he reaches out his hand for mine, and when I offer it, he pulls me into his arms. Not a lover's hug, this is a hug from someone who needs to share his burden with another.

"I knew you were fine, but once I found out, I couldn't get here fast enough."

"How long have you known?"

"James informed the crew about an hour ago. Kathryn was found early this afternoon, but she had to be identified and her family notified before anyone else was told about the incident."

We move to sit on the wicker chairs. The porch is usually a happy place for me to sit, people watch, and reflect. Not tonight. Tonight, it feels sinister and dark.

"My God, I can't believe it. You're sure she was murdered?"

"The police say she was strangled. I don't really know many details. I feel so sad for her, she was a sweet person."

"Strangled…that's awful. Poor Kathryn." Something occurs to me, but I keep it to myself. Maybe she did find Alexandre last night. I think of what Annie told me about a drunk Kathryn, banging on the door, looking for him. I know Alexandre would never do something this sloppy. Never would he leave a body out in the open, and he would never kill an innocent soul. Especially an innocent with such a high profile.

"Strangled. That's all you know? Do you know if she was exsanguinated?" It's risky, but I have to ask.

Jack looks at me like I just escaped from Bedlam.

"What? Do you mean drained of blood? That's a strange, oddly specific question."

"It is strange, for sure. Savannah is a beautiful, but dangerous place, and odd things happen here. A body of a woman who had been exsanguinated was found, a while ago. At least, I think that's what happened. I could be thinking of something else." I could not sound any more stupid if I tried.

"I don't know. If she was, we weren't told."

It's not outside the realm of possibility that this is another senseless, random act of violence. One of many in a city with a very high crime rate. If Kathryn was as drunk as Annie made out and wandering the streets of Savannah alone at night, nothing good could have come of it. The odds are high she merely crossed paths with a psychopath. She was a woman in the wrong place at the wrong time. There is much more to fear from one's fellow man than from any monster, real or imaginary. The depravity of human beings is staggering, and they're afraid of us.

I can tell there is something Jack wants to ask. He is squirming in his seat, running his palms down his thighs, as if they are sweaty. His foot once again, tapping. I figure he wants to ask me about Alexandre. I'm wondering if the cops will show up here looking for him. Wonderful.

"I have to ask you something," he begins, "I don't want to upset you, Millicent, but was Alexandre here last night?"

The easy answer is always the truth, but I can't offer the easy answer right now. Not when this unwanted light is going to shine on all of us. So, I lie.

"I believe so. I thought I heard him in his room last night, but I didn't speak to him. I went straight to bed." I try to tell myself it's only a partial lie. It's all a coincidence, anyway. I feel terribly for Kathryn, but I can't let this expose us.

I can't help thinking, a little selfishly, this throws a big wrench into my plans. If you can call my random thoughts and ideas, plans. What does this mean for Jack? Will production cease, or will they recast? If production of the film halts, Jack will leave, and soon. It's probably not a good time to ask him about it, though. My love life is not as important as a woman's senseless murder.

Jack startles me out of my reverie. "Is he here now? I guess not since no one came to the door."

"No, I'm not sure where he is."

More and more, I'm coming to the realization that this would be a lot simpler if Jack knew about us. I just don't know how to make the transition from, "sorry your friend was murdered," to, "guess what? I'm a vampire." And truthfully, Jack isn't the only one wondering where Alexandre is.

I suggest we go inside, so I can call him. After being intimate with Kathryn, he at least deserves to know. Although, I'm sure he already does, being sensitive to my thoughts and feelings.

I leave Jack in the kitchen with a glass of scotch and run upstairs to get my phone. There's no need to call Alexandre, he has called me, probably when Jack and I were on the porch, and left a voicemail. He informs me that he knows about Ms. Hart, and is as shocked as I am. He decided not to go out of town, has found a new friend, and was visiting with her last night. *Insert eye roll.* Alexandre has already received a call from the police and is heading there now to get this over with. He adds that I am not to worry, and the sooner these movie people are gone, the better. I get his point. He still expects me to break it off with Jack.

It is also glaringly obvious I need to do a better job of shielding my thoughts from him. It won't be easy, as I'm unpracticed, but it is necessary. At least, until we figure all this out.

I return to Jack, telling him about Alexandre's message.

He makes a face, then looks into his glass, "So, he is already with someone else? Ok." Jack pauses, downing his drink in one gulp, "I think I'll go back to the hotel. I need to think and lie down."

"Sure, I understand. I can go with you, so you're not alone."

DEEPEST MIDNIGHT

"That's ok, I want to be alone for a while. I'll call you."

I know he is grieving, but I can't help but feel hurt. He now doesn't want to be with me, when earlier he couldn't get to me fast enough. It seems a quick change of heart. I can't help but wonder what he's thinking. Something to do with Alexandre, I'm sure.

***

Fall 1779, Burgundy Region, France

It felt as if I'd fallen asleep. My limbs are heavy, my eyelids won't open. But, something was happening. I was no longer lying in bed.

"Open your eyes, my dear."

At first, I thought it was Charles. I stubbornly keep my eyes shut tight. I couldn't get them open anyway.

"Millicent, open your eyes. You have the power, make it happen."

It isn't Charles, it's him. The savior from my dreams. My own Roman God, Jupiter. I will my eyelids to lift, and my eyes flicker open. I take a step back in surprise, almost losing my balance.

"Oh, I thought I was in my room. How did I come to be outside?" I ask him.

Jupiter laughs, deep and loud. "You are lying down, fast asleep in your room, right at this moment. Shouldn't you know by now how these walks and talks of ours are only dreams?"

"Yes, of course. It's just this dream, feels like less of a dream than the others. I feel more like myself."

"This is because you are nearing the end of your life with Charles, and the beginning of your life with me."

My heart flutters inside my chest. The thought of walking away from my dreary, unhappy life is almost more than I can bear. I was starting to feel as if the time Jupiter had promised, would never come.

"I'm so glad, but why now?"

"As I've told you before, you have to be ready for your new existence, emotionally, as well as physically. If you are not, the majick can go wrong."

Jupiter never explained what he meant by majick. My mind seemed in a daze whenever I was with him, so I never thought to ask why I would be so different once I left Charles. He takes my hand and we walk. Jupiter pulling me gently behind him, down the familiar, comfortable path.

The path is small, barely visible. Thick, dense trees and brush, surround us on both sides. The moon is bright and full overhead, making the path easily visible. The only sound is the soft wind rustling the leaves.

"How can the majick go wrong?"

I am slightly afraid to question him, but feel something is dangerous about this man. Even though the question was asked, I did not expect him to answer.

"In many ways. It can change you from a lovely woman, into a fierce, wild beast. It can ruin your mind, leaving you without any mental faculties for an eternity."

I stop walking and pull back, "You never told me this, before. I don't understand what you're saying."

"It never came up, before now."

Jupiter turns around, placing his hands lightly on my shoulders. I look up into his crystal eyes.

"Don't concern yourself, right now. I have been planning for this, Millicent. Planning for you. I won't let harm come to you. You can always trust me."

I do trust him. I trust him as I have never trusted any man before. One more question lingers in my mind, another question I had yet to ask.

"What will you want of me once you have used your majick?"

He kisses me sweetly on the forehead and steps back.

"Nothing more than for you to be my companion through the ages. You and only you, will set any other terms. We will make quite the pair."

His eyes twinkle in the moonlight, making it impossible not to smile. I feel safe. My protector, my watcher, the man who will change everything. We continue down the path, until we reach the stone cottage.

"This is where you leave me, my sweet. It's important for you to remember the way, you should have it memorized by now." Jupiter kisses my hand.

I try to protest, beg him to let me stay. Instead, I wake in my luxurious room, the place I hate the most. Lying still, I look around at all the finery, just visible with the light of the moon shining outside. Silks, brocades, crystal, and fine furniture surround me. I should have been a happy woman. One day, I thought to myself, one day.

CHAPTER TEN

The sun has yet to set. There is a steady pounding on the front door, followed by the piercingly loud ring of the doorbell. I know it isn't night, because I'm having a hard time opening my eyes, even a crack.

"Police, open up!"

This is not good. Wake up, Millicent, and think for God's sake. If I open the door, the sunlight will sear my skin, like chicken on a barbeque. Not something these people have ever seen before, I'm sure. Only one thing comes to mind, and I'm not positive it will work. I'll just have to cross that bridge when I come to it.

Dragging ass out of bed, I dig out a very unsexy, white fleece robe. My limbs feel like lead weights, as I do my level best to push my arms through the sleeves. My body is not cooperating. Every cell inside me screams to get back into the safety of my bed. More pounding.

I reach my bedroom door. "I'm coming!"

Not very demure, but it's better than having the door broken in. Since my legs aren't working too well, I slide with locked knees down several steps, almost toppling over in the process.

At the bottom, I robot-walk across the front hall. I stop just long enough to take a deep breath. Gripping the door handle with my left hand, I soundlessly slide back the dead bolt, praying the people outside won't take it upon themselves to try the door, until I am safely removed. I run, awkwardly, into the living room, launching myself onto the sofa, pulling the robe around me.

"Come in!" I yell, hoping they can hear me from outside.

I realize what a stupid idea it is, but what else is a vampire girl supposed to do in the middle of the day?

"Hello?" A woman's voice calls out.

"Yes, hello! Please come in, I'm sick and can't get up!"

Please just open the door and enter. In painfully slow motion, I hear someone place their hand tentatively on the handle of the door, then turn the knob. I'm wondering if they are expecting an explosion or an ambush. Probably can't be too careful. Something much more dangerous lurks inside, but they don't need to know that.

After what seems like hours, but is only a few seconds, the knob is fully turned, and the door is carefully pushed open. I'm doing my best to will my eyes to remain open. If I fall back into a deep sleep, only bad will follow.

"Hello, Savannah PD," says the female voice, again.

"I'm in the living room. I'm sorry, but I'm too sick to get up."

A rather attractive woman in her forties sticks her head into the front hallway, her brown hair brushing her shoulder. I wave from the couch. The woman, wearing a dark suit, takes a look around before walking into the hall. She is quickly joined by a short man, wearing an almost identical suit, and a male officer in uniform. They stand looking at me, for a few uncomfortable seconds. I cough, trying to make my voice sound strained.

"Please come in, I apologize for not being able to answer the door."

The woman in the suit is clearly the person in charge. The short man keeps looking toward her, as if waiting for her cue.

She smiles. "Are you Millicent Mirabeau?"

"That's me."

The woman moves toward me with the other two following close behind. "And is Annie Monroe here, too?" She stands straight as an arrow, hands in her pockets.

"No, I'm not sure where Annie is. She travels quite a lot and comes and goes."

"I see. I'm Detective Addison. This is Detective Wyatt and Officer Thatcher. We would like to ask you a few questions about Kathryn Hart."

Of course, they do. I could kill Alexandre for getting us into this mess.

"I'll answer any questions you have, even though, I only met Kathryn the one time." I sit up, purposely slouching, arms crossed in front of my chest.

"Yes, that's what your cousin said. However, we have to be thorough."

"I understand, ask away."

I have no idea what Alexandre told these people. Therefore, I have no clue how to respond to their questions. I'm guessing the vague truth is the best way to go. Hopefully, it won't get us in trouble. I'm not ready to leave Savannah.

"Let's get right to it, then. Did you notice anything unusual about Ms. Hart the night of your cocktail party?" The two detectives sit opposite me, with the officer looming in the background.

"I wouldn't know what her usual was, so I don't know. She was pleasant and chatty. Nothing about her demeanor seemed odd to me." I don't add that, other than our brief conversation after the party, I barely noticed her that night.

"What was her behavior with your cousin and the director, James Montgomery, like?"

"I'm not sure what you mean," I answer, knowing exactly what she means.

"How was she interacting with them? Was she warm? Cold?"

"Uh, I couldn't say. We were all talking and interacting as a group. I didn't notice Kathryn single anyone out. Are you asking if she was flirting?"

"Your word, not mine. Was she?"

"Not particularly. Like I said, we were all conversing together. I didn't notice anything outside the normal realm of social conversation."

Detective Wyatt is taking a copious number of notes. I feel this must be some sort of tactic, as I haven't said anything of value. Grocery list maybe?

Detective Addison nods her head and regards me with warm, brown eyes. "Interesting."

Nothing I have said is the least bit interesting, unhelpful would be a better word. I wonder if she's using a detective, mind-trick on me.

"Is there anything else you can think of we should know about the night of the party?"

"Truly detective, not a single thing. It was pretty lame, as far as parties go."

She continues to nod, then asks, "Where was your cousin the night of Ms. Hart's death?"

I tell the same lie I told Jack, only I make it more forceful, so there can be no mistaken interpretation. "He was here, all night."

"You're sure about that?"

"Yes, we all turned in early that evening," I answer, without so much as a blink of my eyes.

"What do you know of James Montgomery?"

"Absolutely nothing," I say, getting tired of questions I clearly don't have answers for.

"What was his demeanor at your party?"

"Quiet, but not strange. I imagine as a director, he's used to letting his stars shine, while he hangs out in the background."

Still more nodding. She was starting to make me dizzy.

"Well, Ms. Mirabeau, I don't have any more questions for you, at the moment. I thank you for taking the time to talk with us, today."

"Anytime, detective. I won't shake your hand, as you don't want what I've got."

"I appreciate that." She reaches into her breast pocket, and pulls out a card, "If you have any questions, or can think of something else, please call me."

She places the card on the table, as she and her partner stand to leave, "Thanks, again. We'll see ourselves out."

After their departure, I haul myself to the door, latch it, and then crawl up the stairs. I cross the threshold to my room on hands and knees but am unable to make it to my bed. It's lights out as soon as my heavy, trembling body makes it through the doorway.

I wake with a start to the sensation of floating through air.

"Relax, it's just me."

Alexandre has scooped me off the floor and is in the process of carrying me to my bed.

"The floor is an odd place to sleep, Mills. What's that about?"

"Oh, it's not about anything really. Just had the cops show up here in the middle of the day, and I was forced to let them in."

"How did that work out?" Alexandre asks with a chuckle.

"Not well, obviously. Where have you been and what the hell have you been up to?"

For that line of questioning, Alexandre unceremoniously drops me on the bed. "You know, Mills. A little bit of this and that."

"That's not a good enough explanation, Alexandre."

He shrugs his shoulders, not bothering to say anything else. Clearly the conversation is over for him, but I can't let him off quite so easy.

"Fine, we at least need to talk about the police situation. What did you tell them? I want to make sure our stories line up," I reason.

"Mills, you are too consumed by these mortals and their pitiful existences. Who cares if our stories match? We could kill them all in an instant, and they would never be able to so much as touch us."

"Not funny, you would never be able to slaughter all those innocent people."

He stands there looking at me, not saying a word.

"Right?" I press.

"Right, Mills," he says, with a smirk.

"Stop it. Can you be serious for once? I guess at the very least, if something comes up, we could pack a bag and disappear."

"Now you're getting it. We can do whatever we want. Don't worry about these mortals and their insignificant dramas."

"Ok. You're right," I admit, dearly hating to do so.

"I always am."

Just as I'm about to make a smart aleck remark, I hear someone open the front door. Alexandre hears it at the same time.

"That isn't Annie," he says, taking off toward the stairs.

Why can't he lock the door like a normal person? This isn't 1780. I think it must be the police again, or possibly Jack. That thought alone, compels me down the stairs. I promptly see, I'm wrong on both counts. It's James, and if it's at all possible, he looks even worse than the last time I saw him. The crazy look in his eye has been replaced by something raw and desperate. Alexandre is holding up his hands, telling the wild director to calm down.

"Calm down? I am calm, and I know, I know what happened."

This small, disheveled man is looking dead at Alexandre without so much as a sliver of fear.

"If you're thinking I had something to do with Kathryn's tragic death, you are deeply mistaken. I could never hurt a woman in any way, let alone in the way Kathryn died."

I knew Alexandre was being truthful. We had been constant companions for a long time. I had only ever seen him kill the evil, the wicked. Yes, there had been an exception or two, over the years. When a vampire is starved and the food source is limited, we do what we have to do in order to survive. But, the general rule is followed, by all of us.

James reaches behind him into the waistband of his pants and pulls out a gun, aiming it squarely at Alexandre. I can see right away, from the look in Alexandre's eye, that this is about to go very badly for James. All we need is two dead Hollywood people. I hold up both hands in front of me, staying where I am.

"Millicent, you are free to go. Please leave now," James says, without taking his eyes off Alexandre.

"I can't do that, James," I try to keep my voice as soft, as possible. "I can vouch for Alexandre. He would never murder anyone. I have known him all my life. Please, we have already faced one tragedy, let's not add to it. If you do this, you'd be no better than the person who killed Kathryn. Your life would be over, too. This isn't who you are."

"My life is already over. It ended the night Kathryn died," his voice breaks, as tears spill down his cheeks.

"If anyone understands what you're feeling, it's me," I say.

"Oh, really? How is that?" asks James, as he wipes his eyes with his free hand.

"I lost the love of my life several years ago. I've never been the same, I can't lie to you about that. But, I have learned to go on. You will, too. It will take time, but you will. One day, you will even wake up feeling a measure of happiness again," I pause, letting my words sink in. "I know it doesn't seem like it now, but your grief will lift. I promise."

James' hand is no longer steady but shaking. Deep sobs wrack his body. He drops to his knees, the gun skittering across the hardwood floor. Alexandre grabs the gun as I grab James. Alexandre leaves us on the floor, going back upstairs. Sitting there, on the hard, uncomfortable floor of the hall, we talk quietly for some time.

After James leaves, I lock the door and walk sadly up the stairs. I find Alexandre, sitting on the window seat in his darkly painted room. I lean back against the doorframe.

"You believe I didn't kill her. Right, Mills?"

"Of course, I believe you. You may irritate me more than anyone else but give me some credit."

"Things have been so peculiar, lately. I feel as if you are drifting farther and farther away from me." His voice is unusually sad.

"I'm here, Alexandre. Maybe, stop trying to push me away with your insane behavior, for a start."

"I hate these mortals. I want to leave. I want us to leave. I still expect you to do what I've asked. Tonight, changes nothing."

"I don't understand your insistence upon this," I say, my annoyance with Alexandre, rising.

"I don't wish to discuss it further. I will only say this one last thing. Thank you for the lies you told that idiot downstairs. You handled yourself well."

"What lies? Everything I said was the truth."

"You told him that you had learned to move on from your grief. We all know what a whopper of an untruth that is."

Alexandre's mood shifted drastically from his earlier playfulness. His eyes are sharp, his body rigid. Without another word, I turn around, go into my room and slam the door behind me. I check my phone for a message from Jack. Nothing. Maybe taking off with Alexandre isn't such a bad idea, after all. A lot of good things have happened since I met Jack. A lot of bad things, too.

I need to decompress with a good feeding, followed by a steaming bath filled with lavender bubbles. I'm not going to stare at my phone like a lovesick teenager.

CLARA WINTER

CHAPTER ELEVEN

The next evening, my phone vibrates on the bedside table, where it sits on top of the book Jack gave me. My phone has never seen this much activity; Annie being the only one who ever calls or texts. It's a relief to see the call is from Jack. I was a little nervous, wondering when I would hear from him again. He wants to come over. His voice sounds tired, strained.

"I'm here, whenever you want to come by."

I shouldn't be worried, but that's a lie. Worrying was always a part of my mortal life. It's a part of me, once again. Truthfully, I'm more than worried, I'm scared. There was another note in Jack's voice. Something I can't quite put my finger on. My gut tells me he wants to talk about more than Kathryn's murder. This could be the end to our relationship.

All I can do is move forward and hope for the best. I will let him lead the conversation and see where it goes. If Jack wants to continue, whatever this is, I will figure out how to reveal myself and let the chips fall where they may. If his plan is to end it with me, my heart will once again be broken, but I won't put that on Jack. Moving through the centuries alone, is daunting to say the least, but it's not like I haven't already been there, done that.

Alexandre would call me cowardly and weak...maybe he's right. I've never been good at the whole vampire thing. It's something I'm truly tired of. If only I could stand strong on my own. I could choose to be the master of my own fate, deciding for myself how I feel. Keeping away the dark depression, would be a beautiful thing.

Kathryn's death caused quite the media sensation. It's not every day a star of her caliber is found strangled in a cemetery. News vans quickly moved in and can be seen driving every which way. Looking out my bedroom window, I spot three of the logo-emblazoned vans, parked along the street in front of my house. Apparently, word has leaked about Ms. Hart's involvement with a wealthy local, shortly before her death. This sensationalism will bring a lot of unwanted attention to Savannah, which no one here needs. This is a place where secrets go to die. Who knows what may be dredged up now.

When Jack arrives, I open the door and he quickly ducks in.

"We need to talk," is all he says.

Talking usually ruins everything, but I keep this to myself.

"Sure." I try to sound as nonchalant as possible.

Jack walks into the living room and I follow, making a note he didn't take my hand. I offer him a drink, which he declines. We find ourselves, once again, on the love seat. This time feels very different.

"What's on your mind? Is there news about Kathryn?" I ask, thinking we may as well rip off the Band-Aid and get on with it.

"To be honest, a lot is on my mind. And no, nothing yet."

"Ok. How are you doing with this? And everyone else? I can't imagine what it must be like."

"It's strange. None of the cast or crew knew her well. I certainly didn't. James had worked with her before, may even have been involved with her at some point. He's clearly devastated. He doesn't want to re-cast her part and I can't say I blame him. We will be packing up and going home as soon as everyone is cleared by police."

"Of course." I swallow hard, waiting for what comes next.

"But I didn't come here to talk about Kathryn. My time in Savannah is ending and I don't want to leave without knowing where we stand. With you constantly running out on me, I haven't been able to gauge your feelings. When this first began you said you just wanted to have fun. Regardless of how you feel, I'm going to clarify my feelings for you and tell you what I want."

This is the first-time Jack has taken the reins with me, leaving me relieved.

DEEPEST MIDNIGHT

I take his hands. "I want to know how you feel, so please tell me."

"Honestly, Millicent, your running out bothers me. I'm not sure what the story is. Maybe you have something to hide or maybe you've been hurt by other men. The truth is you have sent an electric current through my life. I'm thirty-eight years old and have never known a woman so magnetic. I want what we have to continue. Frankly, I want more from you." Jack smiles, takes a breath and continues, "that was a lot for me. Now, I need to know what you're thinking."

I push him back against the loveseat, straddle his waist and plant a long, deep kiss on his mouth. Pulling back, I sit on his thighs. "I feel the same way."

He puts his arms around my rear, pulling me in a little closer.

"I don't want this to end either. I'm sorry for making you feel as if I was running away from you." Pausing, I bite my lip, unsure of how to continue. "There are some things you need to know that may change how you want to proceed."

He sighs. "I was afraid of that. Is it Alexandre? Honestly, I haven't been sure of him from the beginning and there is his relationship with Kathryn to consider, as well."

I cover my mouth to keep from laughing. "Let's take one thing at a time. Alexandre and me? Together?"

He shrugs. "I've considered it over the last couple of weeks. I didn't like the way he was looking at me during the cocktail party, like he wanted to stab me. At this point, I don't think anything will surprise me."

"Just so we're clear--I'm not involved with Alexandre or anyone else." Jack's shoulders visibly relax. "And regarding Kathryn, if you're thinking he hurt her, he would never do something like that. I've lived with the man most of my life, and he wouldn't hurt a fly. James however, was clearly obsessed, unbalanced, and much more likely, if you want me to point out suspects."

James' breakdown yesterday, mostly convinced me of his innocence. But, I need to throw suspicion off of Alexandre.

He shakes his head vehemently. "No way. You're reaching. He genuinely cared for her."

"Right, I'm sure he did. Maybe, they don't have crimes of passion in England?" I move off his lap, annoyed.

"I guess you have a point, there," he pauses. "That poor girl. No matter what, she didn't deserve her fate."

I take his hand, "No, she didn't."

"Unfortunately, there's nothing we can do for Kathryn now, and this isn't helping. The police will find her killer. Let's talk about us moving forward. You said there are things I need to know. Like what?"

"I need to show you. After all, seeing is believing."

He looks genuinely perplexed.

"How am I going to do this?" speaking more to myself than him.

"Do what?" His shoulders are tense again.

"Come into the kitchen with me."

I jump up, taking his hand. Maybe Annie was on to something. It may be gruesome, but how else am I supposed to do this? He'll never believe me if I tell him. Sometimes you have to see the unbelievable in order to believe it.

Jack doesn't say anything as we go through the door to the kitchen. Telling him to sit on the stool, I move around the counter, so we are facing each other. I select a small paring knife from the knife block and set it next to the sink.

"Are you squeamish around blood?"

"Why? Is this where the stabbing happens? Is Alexandre behind me?" He's trying to be humorous but is clearly getting nervous, his foot taps wildly.

"Jack, I can't really think of any other way to do this. I've never done it before."

"Done what? You're freaking me out, Millicent."

My eyes are steady on his. "I've never revealed myself to a human before." I pause, letting that sink in for a moment.

Jack laughs uncomfortably. "What the hell are you talking about, Millicent? Did you just lose your mind, or did I? A human?"

This may not go well. However, I have gone too far to stop now. I've no choice but to continue and hope this all comes together.

"You hate it when I leave before dawn. Did you ever wonder if there was a specific reason why? Have you ever wondered why I'm so cold to the touch?"

Now, I've succeeded in making him think I'm insane. The look on his face says it all, but something is registering.

"Are you going to tell me you're a vampire? Jesus, Millicent. You can just say you didn't want to stay with me."

He puts his hands on the counter, about to push himself up. I put my hands on top of his, maybe a bit too forcefully. "Sit down and watch. I'm not crazy, but in a minute, you may *think* you are."

We stare each other down for a few seconds. Finally, Jack resumes his seat. So blindingly fast, he can't even see me move, I grab the knife with my right hand and slice into my left forearm.

Jack grips the counter with one hand and covers his mouth with the other. I think he may scream or be sick, but he doesn't move or make a sound. His eyes are big as saucers as he stares at my left arm. I'm holding it over the sink to catch the blood that pours out. It isn't necessary for long as the deep wound knits itself back together in seconds.

Jack, eyes wide and with his hand still over his mouth, leans in for a closer look. He sees what's happening, but it's hard to tell what's real. When the wound has fully healed, I wet a towel and sponge off the blood that still lingers on my arm. Revealed underneath is perfect, untouched skin. Jack leans over the counter, grabbing my arm. He reaches out with his other hand and feels the skin, turning and twisting my arm to see all sides. I wait silently for him to process what he's seen.

"It's not possible," he whispers.

"It is. Open your mind and accept it. The world is full of the unexplainable, Jack. I think you know that, don't you?"

He releases my arm and puts his head in his hands. "Millicent, if you are messing with me, I swear I will leave this house and never speak to you again."

"I wouldn't do that to you. Besides, how could I fake what I did?" I take his hand, giving it a gentle squeeze. I explain how when he called the other night, I was in the bath tub and had to wait until the sun went down, so I could sneak out the back door of my own home.

He looks at me. His mind is working again. "The others. Alexandre and Annie?"

"The same as me."

"That's why you asked if Kathryn had been drained of blood?"

"Yes, and that's why I know for a fact Alexandre didn't kill her. Why would he strangle her and not drink her blood? It makes no sense. We also don't harm the innocent, which Kathryn was."

He stares at me with unblinking eyes. I'm afraid he's going to run, instead he nods, closing his eyes. He's probably about half way to believing me.

"There's more and I'm prepared to share it all with you when you're ready. Will you jump down the rabbit hole with me?"

CHAPTER TWELVE

Walking back around the kitchen counter, I approach Jack slowly, hoping he isn't afraid of me. His hands are folded on top of the counter. His eyes stare straight ahead. I can't read anything on his face. Tentatively, I reach out my hand, lightly touching his arm. I'm afraid he is going to flinch, but he doesn't. He turns his head toward me, followed by his body. Jack reaches up and touches my cheek. His gesture makes me think he may actually accept all of this.

If only our life could be this simple--a boy and girl in love--the end. The only ending I ever wanted.

"I'm guessing you're actually much older than I am. How old are you?"

Not what I expected, but I'll take it. I won't make a joke about how he shouldn't ask a lady her age.

"Two hundred sixty-one, to be exact."

After a few minutes of silence, I ask if he would like that drink now, which he readily accepts.

Taking my time, I pour him a scotch over ice. He needs a minute to take everything in, and I try to give it to him. I'm wondering if I should go for it, telling him the rest of the story, or wait, letting him process one thing at a time.

Setting the drink in front of him, I sit down on the next stool. I want so badly to wrap my arms around him and press my lips against his, but I hold off. If I hadn't told him, we would have had to part very soon. At least this way, we can move on with some honesty.

Jack continues to remain silent and I can't take it anymore. "Jack, can you tell me what you're thinking?"

"I'm not sure where to start. You said you've never revealed yourself to a human before. It's very weird to say that, by the way. Why me?"

"I have real feelings for you. Feelings, I haven't had since becoming immortal. The only way to have an actual relationship was to tell you."

"And, in all the years you've been a vampire, you've never felt this way for another person?"

"Never. You're very special to me, Jack."

He looks me in the eye as he hooks his arm around my waist, tugging me toward him. He crushes his lips against mine. In that moment, I know I did the right thing. He needed to know. There was no way to hide it any longer. What I feel for him is more than desire. Although, right now, desire is winning out.

Pulling back, he says, "I have more questions."

"They can wait," I say, as I pull off my top.

"Yes, they can," he agrees.

We stand, kicking the stools out of the way. Kissing deeply, I unbutton Jack's pants. We both seem to know what we want and get right to it. You would think this would be a bit awkward, but we have it down. Jack pulls away, peeling off my jeans and panties. His jeans come off next. He's going commando and I wonder if he was dressing for convenience. He pushes me, not too gently, against the counter and lifts me up, hands under my buttocks for support.

Usually, he takes his time with me, but in this moment, we're both urgent. Maybe it's the violence he just witnessed or the overall danger of the situation, either way, I'm good with it. When he enters me, I cry out with pleasure and guide his back side with my hands. He takes me wildly, with an abandon that makes my head spin. It doesn't take me too long to climax, loudly. It's a very good thing the house is empty. Jack follows me, moments later. We are spent and breathing heavily. Jack sets me gently back on my feet and takes my face in his hands.

"You are incredible." He gives me a sweet, tender kiss.

I tell him to ask me anything he wants. We decide the best place to talk will be in my bed, after a quick cleanup.

DEEPEST MIDNIGHT

Once we are all cozy, Jack opens the discussion, "You keep saying human as if it's something apart from yourself. So, you'd describe yourself as a vampire? These things are not getting any easier to say out loud, by the way."

"You'll get used to it. I'm not human, I'm immortal and that's how we refer to ourselves, as immortals. We don't care for the term vampire, mostly because of all the pop culture nonsense. The word vampire has become a joke in the modern world. The word no longer inspires the proper fear and respect, the way it used too."

"Immortal." Jack sounds like he is trying to convince himself. Jack rubs the back of his neck, as he stares at the ceiling. "This is truly unbelievable. However, it explains a lot. There were things about you I thought odd. Now, I know why."

I try not to be offended. "Odd? Like what?"

Jack chuckles, "Well, putting aside the fact that I've never seen you in the daylight, I've also not seen you enter a restroom, other than the times we've showered together. In addition, I've never seen you eat. All things human beings do. You've never asked me to stay here. However, I thought that might have something to do with Alexandre."

"I couldn't ask you to spend the night. Then I'd be stuck in the house with you when the sun rose. Kind of a hard thing to explain how I fall into a deep slumber. And yes, I can't ingest anything solid, my body certainly works differently from yours."

Jack's eyebrows go up, as if a thought has just occurred to him. "So...you drink blood?"

"Yes. But, I don't kill those I drink from. Not usually, anyway." I don't elaborate. No need to go into too much detail too soon. But, he's not having it.

"Usually?"

"We have the power to mesmerize humans and only take enough of their blood to nourish ourselves. Once released, they feel like they just had a dizzy spell, but have no memory of the actual event. It's bad karma to hurt the innocent," I explain, hoping that's enough for now.

He nods, not pressing me any further on what *usually* means.

"How are you feeling about this? Do you still want to be with me, knowing there are hefty complications? We'll never be able to have anything as simple as a lunch date. We'll never have children." I trace circles on his chest.

"This is strange, Millicent. There is no way around it. I'm doing my best. It will take some time getting used to." He turns toward me, fixing me with those piercing, heavenly blue eyes. "Just know that I want you. Human or immortal. I don't see that changing and I'm willing to figure this out alongside you."

He kisses me, again with a passion that leaves me gasping for breath.

"Wait a minute," Jack says. The last thing I want to do is talk right now. "You breathe."

I can't help but laugh. He is certainly observant. "Yes, we breathe more out of habit than an actual need for breath. It would be a dead giveaway if we didn't."

I want to point out my pun, as I would with Annie, but I have other things on my mind.

"I have a feeling that I'm going to be learning a lot from you. More than I already have." He grins slyly and pulls me to him. Jack buries his face in my neck, covering it with kisses sending chills down my spine. We make love again, and I feel as if everything has fallen perfectly into place. I am a woman basking in the sun after centuries in the darkness.

Everything is so easy with Jack. My love for Julien was complicated and dangerous. I was not free in the 18th century to live as I pleased. Divorce was unheard of. Women who slept with men outside of marriage were considered whores, no matter how awful their husbands might be. Feminism was nowhere in sight.

There is the potential mess Alexandre could create. I do my best to ignore the unwanted thought lingering in the back of my mind. I can handle him when the time comes.

After a steamy, delicious shower, Jack reminds me that after I cut my arm, I told him there was more. This serves as a reminder that the night of revelation is far from over.

"Should I be scared?" he asks.

"I hope we are through the scariest part. But yes, there is more. Quite a lot, more. You should know my human story and how I came to be what I am. That part may concern you, as well. And you should brace yourself, it may be hard for you to hear."

"Ok. I'm not sure what that means, but I would love to hear your story. Truth be told, I'm incredibly curious." Jack gives me a half-smile.

I take Jack's hand and lead him back into my bedroom. Once again, I feel nervous. Telling him about my past frightens me more than revealing myself as immortal. Part of me wonders if I should skip over how Jack looks exactly like Julien. I'm not sure how I would feel if Jack told me that he was attracted to me because I remind him of someone else. I need Jack to know everything, I believe he has proven that he can deal with it. We're in this for better or worse.

"Everything ok? You seem hesitant." Jack squeezes my hand.

"I'm good." I squeeze his hand back, then release it.

Moving over to the fireplace, I pull on the black braided cord. Two panels of deep, blue velvet part to reveal my portrait. Although I could never part with the painting, gazing at it day after day is far too painful. I used to keep it under the bed but began to fear the portrait would somehow be ruined. Under a bed is not ideal storage for a painting over two hundred years old. My solution was to hang it on the wall in my bedroom, but keep it covered from my sight.

When I turn around I can see Jack is riveted, his head tilted to the side. He squints his eyes, then looks down like he's trying to grasp a memory just out of reach.

"Have I seen this before? In a museum, or something? It looks familiar." I'm not sure if I should be surprised or not. He goes on, "Wait, that's you, isn't it? Where could I have seen this before?"

"Well, we'll get to that. Yes, this is me. My husband commissioned this portrait during the last few months of my mortal life. The only time I was ever truly happy."

"The only time?" Jack asks.

"Until now, yes," I answer.

CLARA WINTER

CHAPTER THIRTEEN

"I was born in 1756, to a mid-level noble, the Viscount Dubois." I pause, jumping to the part of the story which concerns Jack, explaining this takes place in the last few months of my mortal life.

"I was twenty-four that spring. A duchess invited us to a three-day party on her estate. This woman, Clea, loved art. She had a keen interest in portrait painting. The women in attendance would take painting lessons from a master, while the men bonded over hunting and drinking. I wasn't much of an artist, but gladly jumped at any excuse to change up the drudgery of my day-to-day existence.

Charles had no desire to spend time with me, let alone attend a party that would see us thrown together as a couple. Eight years into our marriage, I had not given him any children. Charles was tiring of me, but we had to keep up appearances to some extent. As the Duke and Duchess were a great family, he sent me to represent our household.

"Tell them I'm too busy with the estate, at the moment, to attend and make my apologies."

"Of course, Charles. I know the Duke will understand." I said, happily helping my ladies' maid pack the jewelry case.

"I'm sure you're happy to get away for a few days. Don't forget you are representing me, remember who you are and behave accordingly."

"I'll behave the way I always do, Charles. Have I given you cause to feel embarrassment?"

"Only in one thing. The one thing that really matters to a man with an estate like mine."

I said nothing, there was no point. Those sorts of comments had plagued me since childhood. I let it fall over me, like all the others.

Although I occasionally did leave the chateau, I wasn't well traveled and could barely contain my excitement at the change in scenery. Little did I know, this party would change the course of my life, forever.

I arrived at the estate looking an absolute mess. There had been heavy rains and the roads were difficult to get through. At one point, my driver tried to insist we return. I urged him to continue. Nothing could keep me from the three days of freedom.

A half mile from the Duchess's estate, a wheel broke. I exited the carriage to walk the remainder of the way, dragging my silk skirts through mud as thick as fudge. My hair had come free from the violent rocking of the carriage, so by the time I arrived on the front steps I was bedraggled, caked in mud to my shins, out of breath, and completely happy. I had also lost one of my satin shoes in the muck, but I was too intent on reaching the front door to stop for a silly shoe."

Jack interrupts me. "This is all so surreal, Millicent. You're telling me you lived during a time I've only read about or seen onscreen."

"I know. I can't imagine how strange this must seem to you."

Jack nods. "It's definitely strange, but I'm fascinated. Go on."

"I told the footman where he could find my carriage and driver, as the Duchess came out to greet me.

"Oh, my dear!" Clea exclaimed, "Are you alright?"

I laughed. "I was determined that nothing would keep me away from you, even the rotten roads."

"Yes, the roads to the south are a mess. The other guests came from the north, which were completely dry. Let's get you to your room."

Clea ignored the serving girl, helping me out of my shoe and sodden stockings, herself. Together, we hiked up my skirts as we walked across the grand foyer. Arm in arm we trudged up the marble staircase to the east wing of the main chateau, where my room was located.

Clea wasn't afraid of a little mud, as she wasn't always a great lady. Her marriage caused a great scandal, at the time. Her husband, the Duke, plucked her out of obscure poverty to make her his mistress. Instead of tiring of her, he fell in love and they married in secret. It took a few years before polite society would accept Clea as an equal, but she triumphed. Her lowly beginning forgotten, she was now one of the greatest, most respected ladies in all of France. One of the only real-life, fairy tale endings I had ever heard of.

Once in my room, which was far grander than my own at home, Clea left me in the capable hands of two maids. One began preparing a bath, while the other helped me out of my ruined dress and underclothes. After a quick bath, I wrapped myself in an enormous blanket, then stepped onto the balcony for some fresh air.

The rains left the air smelling fresh, like grass and barely opened flowers. Birds were chirping happily, I couldn't help but feel happy too. This freedom, though temporary, felt wonderful. I tried not to let it go to my head, but in my heart, I longed for more days like this.

Hearing voices, I looked down. Two ladies and a gentleman stood next to an enormous fountain. I recognized the ladies, both Viscountess's. I turned my attention to the man.

When my gaze fell on him, I was startled to find that he was already watching me. I took a small, quick step back with every intention of darting inside. But, I couldn't take my eyes from his. Somewhat tall, with a regal posture, his copper hair shined in the sunlight. His skin was fair, but not pale. From what I could see at this distance, his eyes looked shockingly like sapphires. Never had a man regarded me with such interest. I felt riveted to my spot.

As I stood there, not moving my gaze from his, my body stirred in a way that was wholly unfamiliar to me. His mouth broke into a wide grin. At that, I snapped myself out of the trance, turned around, practically stumbling back into my room closing the doors sharply behind me.

It was only then I realized I was still wrapped in the blanket and not properly dressed. It occurred to me this was probably the reason for the man's staring. My face flushed with embarrassment, I may as well have been standing outside naked. I thought myself a simple fool as I put on my dressing gown.

Sitting at the vanity, I let my thoughts drift to the man by the fountain. I laughed, shaking my head, what a funny way to begin this adventure; covered in mud one moment, then making a dunce of myself the next.

All of this troubled me very little. Yes, it was embarrassing, but no one else seemed to have noticed me. If this man was a gentleman, which I had to assume he was, he would never mention it. I was still glad to have the freedom of the next three days ahead of me, regardless of anything else. I would gladly face a little humiliation for it."

I pause my story and look up at Jack, who looks as if he is trying to work something out.

"What is it?" I ask.

"The man you just described sounds a little like me, minus the wonderful posture."

"Believe me, I know. Something you want to share?" I ask Jack, who's starting to look a bit anxious, tapping his foot in his telltale way.

"Now I'm the one who's going to start sounding crazy," he says, "Millicent, I felt from the start I knew you. I told myself it was nothing more than the intense attraction I felt for you. Are you telling me that maybe I did know you?"

"Honestly Jack, I don't know. I've been asking myself the same thing from the beginning. The man I described didn't just resemble you, he looked exactly like you. I know people, vampires too, who believe in past lives. I've never had occasion to think about it, until now. I know about as much as you do. Do you want me to continue?"

"More than anything." He says, leaning back in the chair.

"After I had a giggle over my silliness, I called back the maids who had been assigned to me. We began the gargantuan task of hair, makeup, clothing, and jewels. It was time I join the others and could only do so once I had been made to fit the ideal standard of beauty of 18th century France.

I'll never forget what I wore that day. The day dress, a polonaise, simple for its time, was a light, cornflower blue with soft, barely noticeable vertical stripes. Delicately ruffled around the low-cut neckline and at my elbows, where the sleeves ended, the dress was understated elegance. The only jewelry I donned was my diamond wedding band and small pearl ear bobs.

My hostess was kind enough to leave a schedule of the party's events on the bedside table. It was now one o'clock. There would be a wine tasting, with hors d'oeuvres at three, before dinner at seven. That meant I had two hours to become acquainted with the grounds and to see who else was in attendance, besides the man with the gorgeous eyes.

CHAPTER FOURTEEN

"Placing Clea's schedule on top of the bedside table, I made my way toward the front of the room ready to escape, excited to explore. Before I could walk the fifty or so steps to the door, there was a knock. I pulled open the double doors to reveal the Duchess.

"Well, my dear, now that you've had time to recover from your journey, you look absolutely gorgeous. None the worse for wear."

She threw open her arms, enveloping me in a soft hug. Clea smelled like talcum powder, mixed with what I suspected to be a little wine. She was a lovely woman in her fifties with white hair and powdery skin. Clea's average height was filled out nicely by a soft, voluptuous figure. Her ivory day dress, decadently ruffled down the front, was much more elaborate than mine, and lower cut, to emphasize she was still an attractive woman.

"I decided to throw together a tour of the grounds. Are you ready?"

"Of course," I answered, "but, ready for what exactly?"

"One of the guests, my painter, caught a glimpse of you from the verandah. He discreetly inquired as to whether you are married. Apparently, in what was but a moment, you quite entranced the man." She smiled at me. "Of course I told him you are married, enjoying one of the finest and most spotless reputations in all of France. He looked awfully forlorn, but I suspect he will quickly move on to the one lady in attendance who is unattached. So, not to worry, my dear." She linked her arm with mine, patting my hand, as we set off down the hallway.

I was a little stunned. And, if I was being truthful, flattered. I knew my cheeks were flushed but could only hope that my makeup covered my true *feelings.* Her painter also caught my eye. All I could do, however, was shrug it off. Unhappy as I was in my marriage, for me to be unfaithful was unthinkable. The consequences would be severe.

The Duchess and I walked, talking all the while. Our conversation was nothing more than shallow chitchat. It occurred to me there was nothing I wouldn't give for a real escape, alone. Putting on a fake smile, day after day, was exhausting.

The others were gathered on the eastern lawn of the estate. The weather had cleared, and the sun shined brightly. Thankfully, the party was rather a small one. There were two couples, of which I was acquainted, and one single lady, who was a stranger to me. She was young and lovely, with chestnut brown hair, green eyes, and a trim figure. I greeted my acquaintances, then the Duchess introduced me to the young lady, whose name was Eve. As Eve and I were shaking hands, the man Clea had called her painter, walked up to the party.

"Millicent, Marchioness of Mirabeau, allow me to introduce you to Julien Delacroix, master painter."

I couldn't avoid his gaze, and not seem rude. But as I looked directly his eyes, I felt an electric current go through me. Monsieur Delacroix took my hand, bowed over it, and pressed my fingertips to his lips. It was all I could do to keep breathing steadily.

"A great pleasure, my lady." His voice was deep, gravelly, and masculine.

"Thank you, Monsieur, likewise."

When he released my hand, I lowered my eyes and took a step back. His voice was even more hypnotic than his eyes. I let myself imagine, this man in my bed whispering in my ear with that penetrating voice. Warmth spread through my face, and I quickly told myself to think of other things. I didn't know what was coming over me. Surely, this man would treat me no differently in the bedroom then my husband given the chance. The thought quickly sobered me up.

The Duchess called us to attention and began the tour. I was grateful for the distraction. Eve came to walk along side of me. Monsieur Delacroix walked behind us. I tried to keep my focus on what the Duchess was saying.

While Clea was telling her guests the history of her impressive, marble statue of the goddess Aphrodite, I slipped away into a copse of rose bushes. Behind the thicket of roses was a tiny stone cabin. The cabin reminded me of my regular dreams of a man I thought of as Jupiter, and a feeling of safety and belonging came over me. The blooms were fragrantly sweet, the sharp contrast between blood red and snowy white was arresting. I reached to pluck one of the red flowers, when I heard someone come up behind me. Thinking *it must be Clea, I turned with a smile, ready to confess my poaching of her rose.*

I was startled to see it was Monsieur Delacroix, all alone.

"Don't worry Madame, I will not tell on you."

He smiled at me wickedly, as he moved along side of me.

He took my hand in his, reaching it up to stroke the petals. Shocked, I pulled my hand away, ready to turn and leave. But something held me back. Curiosity maybe. More shocking still, Monsieur Delacroix plucked the rose, tucking it in the bust of my dress.

"Monsieur, how dare you touch me."

I pulled out the rose, throwing it on the ground.

"No one is here to see, Madame. Your reputation shall remain...spotless. You could have been Aphrodite yourself, wrapped as you were on the verandah," he said with a laugh, but then abruptly stopped.

I looked stonily into his eyes, refusing to run away.

"I am sorry, Madame, truly. I meant no offense."

We continued to hold each other's gaze for a moment longer. He bent down to pick up the rose, then pressed it gently into my hand. Monsieur Delacroix turned away, leaving me there, more confused than I had ever been in my life.

Rejoining the party in front of the statue, I willed myself to look anywhere but toward him. Our walking tour continued down a gravel path with perfectly groomed hedges on one side, and an expanse of mossy green ground cover on the other. After several minutes of Clea talking about the hedges and how she trims them herself, we turned, to face a little stone bridge, the same stone as the little cabin. From what I could see, the bridge crossed a tranquil stream which looked shallow but was quite wide.

"If we walk over the bridge, we can cross back to our waiting food and drink more quickly. We go two at a time and watch your step, the stones are rather uneven," explained Clea.

Clea took the arm of Eve and the two stepped up onto the bridge. The two couples followed, which left me with Monsieur Delacroix. I felt a panic rise in my chest. What if he reached for my arm? Wearing a veil over my emotions had become second nature for me, but this man had succeeded in making me question everything in the short span of two hours.

"After you, Madame," said Monsieur Delacroix, quietly.

He did not reach out his arm for me. Daintily, I picked up my skirts, stepping up onto the first stone. I continued up the next two stairs, until I almost reached the top. The second my foot descended onto the top of the bridge, it slipped out from under me, toppling my body backward.

Two strong arms plucked me out of mid-air, pulling me into a firm embrace. Relieved to be on solid ground, I didn't pull away.

"You're alright, I have you," his breathy voice whispered against my neck, sending a current straight through me.

My throat constricted. Only two people, my dear Blanche and my dreamy Jupiter had ever spoken to me with such tenderness.

Clea's screeching voice pulled me back into reality.

"Is she hurt?!"

Immediately righting myself, I turned toward Clea. Monsieur Delacroix kept his hand lightly on the small of my back.

"I'm fine, don't fuss. This gentleman saved me from breaking my neck."

"You scared me terribly, dear. Take my hand and let's all finish making our way over this treacherous bridge."

Monsieur Delacroix removed his hand. Suddenly, I felt alone.

After our lengthy walk, we were ushered onto an immense portico. There were several intricately carved, silver vessels, each filled with a different type of wine. Many crystal glasses also littered the large banquet table, along with several delicate and delicious looking finger foods. The guests immediately helped themselves. Monsieur Delacroix poured a glass of wine. Instead of drinking it himself, he handed the glass toward me.

"Madame, if you would."

I took the glass, bringing it to my lips. He took a step closer to me, close enough that I felt the heat from his body. He smelled like paint and sunshine. My breath quickened.

"Madame, let me teach you how to savor wine, properly."

Taking the glass from me and in a gesture, I found too intimate, swirled the glass, breathed in the scent of the liquid, then took a drink.

He handed it back. "Swirl the wine in the glass, and then breathe it in. Tell me what you smell."

I felt incredibly awkward but did as he bid. At first, I smelled nothing but wine. On the second try, I had it."

"Cherries," Jack says, startling me out of my skin.

"How did you…" I begin.

"All of a sudden, I could smell cherries." Jack taps his foot so hard, I'm afraid he may break a toe. "Keep going," He urges.

"Monsieur Delacroix smiled, turning back to the table to fill another glass. I took the opportunity to back into the crowd. Moving to the edge of

the portico, I let my mind wander, as I took in the beauty of the southern grounds.

When I turned back to the crowd, I saw Julien, Monsieur Delacroix, conversing with Eve. She was smiling, laughing at something he was saying. She placed a small, gloved hand on his arm. I couldn't help but feel a pang of jealousy. I felt frustrated, foolish even. Those were not feelings I was accustomed to.

After a few more minutes, the Duchess announced it was time for the ladies to rest before dinner. Setting down my glass, I practically bolted inside, keeping my eyes trained on the ground. I welcomed the solitude with relish.

Once in my room, I flung myself on the bed. Lying there, I began to contemplate feigning illness. Anything to get out of the evening. A rustling sound outside the door reminded me that the ladies' maids were probably coming to help me refresh for the evening. I found it odd, when after several moments, no one knocked or entered.

I walked over. A note had been slipped underneath. It was half under the doorjamb, daring me to pick it up. I was frozen, terrified at what it could say, or from whom it could be. I stooped down to pick up the creamy paper sealed with red wax, stamped with a Fleur de Lis.

Returning to the bed, I slid my finger underneath the seal.

> *"Madame,*
> *Please forgive me. I do not wish to make you uncomfortable. I expect nothing and only wish to convey a few words. Your charms have quite enchanted me. I understand you to be a virtuous wife. I mean no disrespect. However, it is not in my nature to ignore such things. You are not like any woman I have ever met.*
> *Yours, Julien."*

For a moment, I was overwhelmed. Never had anyone said such things to me. Even my own husband was never romantic. These beautiful words made me feel joy, not shame. Smiling the first genuine smile of the day, I folded the note and slipped it into the bottom of my jewelry case.

Ready for the evening, I stood in front of the full-length mirror unable to help but wonder if Julien would be pleased. My robe à la française was a blush pink satin, with buttons of the same color down the front and delicate snow-white lace at the sleeves. The skirt embroidered with swooping, golden birds. My hair was styled in a simple pouf, pinned together in the back, by golden birds that matched my dress. Pink diamonds set in gold adorned my ears, throat, and wrist.

Once downstairs, I was immediately happy with my simpler hair and makeup. The other ladies all donned massive wigs with so much powder on their faces, they looked like corpses with bright pink lips. Looking around the table, I did not see Julien, so I inquired to the Duchess where her painter might be.

"Oh, dear. Monsieur Delacroix was feeling tired and has retired early."

I smiled and said I hoped he would feel better soon. Inwardly, I was bitterly disappointed. In fact, I was shocked at just how keenly the disappointment was felt."

CHAPTER FIFTEEN

I'm ready to continue my story for Jack, but a little sweat seems to be beading at his hairline.

"Can I get you some water?" I ask, starting to feel concern this isn't going well.

Jack is tapping his foot but looks me directly in the eye. "No, I'm okay. Anxious to hear what happens next."

"After dinner, I excused myself early. The Duchess assumed I was still tired from the journey, which worked for me. I was tired, but not in the way she thought. All through dinner, I listened to one insipid conversation after another. I was tired of my shallow life, of not having love, and of putting on a daily performance. With my head, and spirits down, I started the long walk back to my room.

Halfway down the hallway, I raised my head and saw a figure leaning against the wall next to my door. In that moment, I knew exactly what I was going to do. Reputation be damned.

"Good evening, Monsieur." I said, once I had closed the distance between us.

"Madame," he paused, "you will think me presumptuous. I only wanted to say good night, but look at you, you take my breath away."

"Won't you please come in?"

Julien was stunned, his eyes wide. He must have thought I'd be a difficult conquest. Being a well-born gentleman, his visible shock was momentary. He smiled, peering down the hallway past me, I assumed to make sure no one else was about.

I opened the door and entered the room. Julien right behind me. I felt delightfully excited. My breath was shallow, with a not unpleasant nervous twinge in my stomach. He closed the door and I asked him to lock it.

"I admit you have taken me off guard, Madame and have me at a disadvantage, all be it, a happy one. This is not what I expected."

"Let me be frank, Monsieur. This escape is a short one. I'm tired of games, I play them all day, every day. I long to be real with someone, even if it is only this once. And, I think you can call me Millicent."

Just as Julien looked as if he would devour me, I turned away. I might have been ready to jump into bed with a man I just met, but a steadying glass of wine, never hurt anyone. After I poured two glasses, I handed one to him.

"You are very quiet, have you changed your mind?" I ask.

Julien drank down his wine in one gulp. Suddenly, he seemed almost nervous. Perhaps he wasn't quite the ladies' man I thought him to be.

"No, my dear, I have not changed my mind about you. Are you certain this is what you want? You have so much more to lose than I, if anyone were to find out."

"I am sure," I reassured him. "I fear being discovered, of course. What scares me more is living a life that has never once known desire."

He nodded. "Ah. Your husband never showed you what pleasure is. In many ways, this will be like your first time."

I looked away, suddenly ashamed of myself.

"Please don't look away. You've nothing to feel shame for. This is your husband's shame, not yours. Had he so wished, he could have made you happy. But then, if he had, perhaps I would not be faced with such an honor now."

Julien moved swiftly toward me. His eyes on mine. He took the wine glass from me, setting it on the table. Without a word, he began to remove my jewelry, quickly but with care. All the while, I could only look at his face, his eyes, his mouth. His fingers softly brushed my neck, only for a moment, which was maddening. Finished with this task, he unpinned my hair, sending my blonde curls, tumbling down my back.

His deep, blue eyes locked with mine. "Don't be nervous."

"I'm not."

I was telling the truth since all unease had left. Only desire so acute remained. It was almost painful. This was a new sensation for me, I had never felt anything but revulsion during this act. I suddenly knew what desire was, and I never wanted to go without it again.

I gripped his waistcoat, drawing him nearer. In a flash, Julien had my face in his hands, his mouth on mine. With our mouths open and my tongue sliding over his, I was feverish. There was no slow burn, rather I felt as if my whole body were his for the taking. I tried to only feel the physical sensation. I didn't want to feel emotionally close to him, but I feared that I would fail in this, miserably.

It felt like it took an eternity to peel off the layers of our clothing. We fell into the bed. With one hand on my lower back, pressing me to him, and one hand massaging my breast, he began to kiss his way down my neck. I felt as if I was coming to life. Julien continued to kiss and lick his way down my body, pausing to lave at my breasts. My head swam as he closed his mouth over my sex, sucking and licking. I never knew I could feel such intense pleasure. With my hand on the back of his head, I began to move my hips. I no longer had any control over myself.

I moaned, arching my back. With his hands, he reached around and grasped my buttocks, pushing himself into me. Before I knew what was happening, I felt a tidal wave of pleasure crashing through my body in a jerking spasm. I cried out as Julien wrung out every drop of my orgasm. Pushing back, he crawled his way up my body. I pulled his mouth to mine as he entered me. I moaned in delight. We moved in time together, hands everywhere, mouth on my face and neck. Moments later I was crying out, again in pleasure, and this time Julien was crying out with me.

My lover collapsed in a heap by my side. My legs felt deliciously numb, and I tingled all over. Had anyone tried to explain this to me, I would have thought them liars. To feel such intense passion and joy, it was overwhelming.

We made love twice more, before Julien rose to leave. I could make love with him for an eternity. Alas, he had to leave before the household began to stir. Knowing this didn't make it any easier to let him go.

"My darling, sleep now, and I will see you at breakfast. It will take all my strength not to sweep you up in my arms." He slipped on his shoes, knelt on the bed, and swooped down to kiss me.

"It will be torture," I said, half asleep already."

Jack interrupts me, again. "You were prepared to give up everything for him, after having just met him? You must have been painfully unhappy."

"I was. I know it must seem crazy, but I wasn't living a real life. My life didn't truly begin until I met Julien."

"It doesn't seem crazy. He came into your life at just the right moment." Jack continues tapping away with his foot, but he also smiles then nods for me to continue.

The day was a painfully slow one. Julien and I put on our best show, no one seemed to have guessed what had taken place.

Once night had arrived, and as soon as it was safe, Julien was in my bed once more. Our second night was in no way diminished, instead, it was better.

As Julien was once again preparing to leave me, I couldn't help but say, "Only one more night."

Words could not express the anguish I felt. Julien, sitting on the edge of the bed, dropped his head into his hands.

"I have doomed myself, Millicent. I knew when I saw you, you would be the end of me if I allowed it, and I have."

I sat behind him, wrapping my arms around his chest.

"You're not the one who must return to a dreaded husband, at least you are free. What can we do?"

"We will think of something, for I know now I cannot be without you."

My heart soared at his words. His love was all I ever wanted, and I had finally found it. Looming over all this delirious happiness was the specter of my husband, complete with a life I could not choose for myself.

During the mid-morning painting lesson, where Julien and I had to once again play act at being strangers, Clea leaned over to look at my canvas.

"Don't look, it's awful," I laughed.

"Oh, it's not so bad, you just need more lessons. You must have Charles commission Monsieur Delacroix to paint your portrait. While at your chateau, he can continue to teach you."

I felt as if I could fly. "Clea, you are a genius."

I kissed her on both cheeks. She laughed and told me I was a silly girl. Perhaps I was, but I now knew how to prolong my affair. I would take as much time as I could get.

That night, our last at Clea's chateau, I told Julien my plan. He liked the idea but was uncertain we could continue our liaison under my husband's nose.

"It is still only a temporary reprieve, we must be even more careful. It will be dangerous. Surely your husband will have his eye on us. However, at least we can be together, and this will buy us some time to make a more permanent plan."

"Permanent?" Unable to believe my ears, I held my breath.

"Yes, my love. You are it for me, the only woman I have ever felt so deeply for. It may seem foolish, after so short a time, but I speak from the heart. My dream would be to make you my wife, but it is extremely unlikely your husband would allow you a divorce, as you've said. The only solution I see, is running away together and leaving the country. I have thought all day about this, and how we can make a living. It will be a hardship for you. But, painting your portrait will allow us some time to think on this further."

My heart leapt at his words. Julien had been thinking of how we could be together, always. This was more than I had dreamt to hope for. To run away with him sounded so romantic. I would be giving up a lavish lifestyle, but I would gladly have lived in a cave if it meant spending my life with him. I never felt our choice was rash. Instead, I felt as if for the first time I was being true to myself. Julien's last name, Delacroix, means those who live at a crossroads. That was certainly where we found ourselves.

The plan was for me to return home, gush about the fabulous portrait Julien painted of Clea, and how everyone who was anyone, wanted one of their own. My vain husband would not be able to resist. Charles would feel he too must have a portrait of his wife painted immediately. Bragging about how he secured the most up and coming painter in all of France to paint his wife, would give Charles a new reason to be proud of himself. The portrait would become a centerpiece, another item Charles could point at, to show off his wealth and brilliance.

Before leaving me early our last morning, Julien removed the gold band he wore on his little finger and placed it on the ring finger of my right hand.

"This was my mother's ring. One day soon, I will move it to your left hand."

Leaving him was painful, a cold fear sat in my belly. I attributed it to the uncertainty of our future. But, once I arrived home, everything went exactly as I had predicted. I told Charles about Monsieur Delacroix, how the others in attendance over the weekend were attempting to outbid each other, hoping to secure the honor of a portrait painted by him.

"Charles, you should see the portrait of Clea. It is exquisitely beautiful. Everyone wants a painting by this Delacroix."

My ridiculous husband practically fell over himself getting to his desk.

"No one shall outbid me. This painter shall be here in a fortnight."

Charles was true to his word. This was the one and only time during our marriage when I was pleased with him. Of course, he had no idea where my real pleasure in all this lay.

Julien arrived at the chateau precisely thirteen days after I had. If I was a superstitious woman, this may have made me anxious. As it was, nothing could dampen my spirits.

When the carriage bearing my love pulled up to the front of the drive, I could barely contain my excitement. I wanted to run to him, to drag him upstairs. Instead I kept my hands clasped tightly behind my back. My usual veil of serenity in place.

Charles was in the stable, overseeing the breeding of a new thoroughbred. He wouldn't bother himself with someone as lowly as a painter. The less time he spent with us, the better.

Our nightly rendezvous continued. I feigned a cough, to keep Charles from my room. The man was terrified of illness to the point of mental distress, so this was easily done. However, this hardly seemed necessary, as Charles had not visited me once since my return. I hoped this meant he was no longer interested, or perhaps it meant he had a lover of his own. Either way, it was a win for me. About a week after Julien's arrival, Charles left on extended business. Our plan was working perfectly.

We enjoyed bliss for seven weeks, constantly in each other's company. Our days were spent in the bright, airy conservatory, where Julien had set up his studio. We would only break for meal times and a daily walk of the grounds. In the evening, I would make my way silently to his room. We felt this was the safest course of action, as I could more readily find an excuse for walking around my own home in the middle of the night. It began to feel a little too easy, too comfortable.

One evening, after an exhausting day of painting for Julien, I was about to make my way to his rooms. I was heady with excitement, even though I had done this at least a dozen times. Lighting a small candle, I gently opened my door, then crept as quietly as a mouse, to the room of my love. A sound on the staircase startled me. I blew out the candle and pressed myself against a wall. My heart beat, unsteadily, while I waited to see if someone was there. However, the sound proved to be nothing. I felt a little thrill and smiled to myself.

Seeing would be more difficult now. I wasn't worried, I knew every inch of this hallway. When I had, at last, closed Julien's door behind me, I tossed the unlit candle on a table. Slipping into his bed, I moved up behind him, placing my hand on his chest. He was fast asleep. I couldn't help but be amused. I told him he was working himself too hard.

I felt the sweetness of this moment. Cuddling in, even closer, I lay my head down next to his.

"You fell asleep." Jack jumps up. "Why do I know these things, Millicent? I don't believe in past lives."

I don't want to point out he didn't believe in vampires until tonight, but I keep my teasing to myself.

"I'm not sure what you want me to say, Jack. Should we stop for now?"

He rubs at his eyes. "No, no."

Jack gestures sharply with his hand for me to go on. He is freaking out, but I continue.

Upon waking, I knew I made a mistake. I never fell asleep in his room, it was too risky.

Julien stirred, turning toward me. "Darling, it's morning. What happened?"

"Clearly, I fell asleep," I said, a tad snappishly. "I'm sorry. You were sleeping, I just wanted to lie with you, for a moment. What do I do?"

"Hold on." Julien opened his door and peered down the hallway. "Hurry," he said, beckoning me forward.

He kissed me quickly, then ushered me out. "Silly girl. I'll see you for breakfast."

I swiftly walked down the long hall, thankfully reaching my room without incident.

Before I could open the door, it was opened for me.

"My lady, there you are," said my maid.

"Yes, I thought I heard a strange noise and went to look about."

"Yes, my lady," she answered.

She was too smart a girl to ask any questions, still I had to wonder how much she knew.

During this time, our love deepened. We spoke often of what we would do, when the time came. Trying to secure a divorce was impossible, and therefore out. I would have no grounds, save my own infidelity. The only thing I could count on was being shamed, stripped of my fortune and reputation. Charles would, very likely, send me to a convent or throw me out on the streets.

The only real option, was to run away. Far away, where we could start over. I was ready to leave immediately. But, Julian felt his portrait of me would be his masterpiece, inspired as never before by the love he felt for the subject. He needed to see it finished. I reluctantly agreed, calming my fears by dreaming of our future.

We would never be able to legally marry, but if we ran far enough, changing our identities, which wasn't difficult in a non-technological age, we could pretend to be whoever we wanted. In the meantime, I would hoard as much of my own money and gold, as I could. Taking my jewels to sell, would also give us a good amount of money to live on.

I was not the only one giving up everything. Julien was a new favorite at court, he had come a long way in his life. We were both making sacrifices and were both happy to do so.

As our second month together at the chateau was coming to an end, I had news both exciting and terrifying. I was with child."

CHAPTER SIXTEEN

"Having just turned twenty-four, and having been married for eight years, I had long thought myself unable to conceive a child. Of course, Charles preferred the sensitive term, defective. Oddly, I only thought of the tea when I was in my dreamlike state with the man I knew as Jupiter. Even though I drank it faithfully, it was almost a mindless automation. This act never entered my waking consciousness. I never drank it after being with Julien.

I knew this would cause a few problems, but I felt such joy that any negative thought was quickly squelched. It would all work out, it had too. All sorts of new beginnings were in sight. To reveal my pregnancy to Julien, required the perfect moment. I decided the moment would be dinner, the week after I missed my course.

"Millicent, you keep dropping your chin."

Julien was working at a fast pace, but not fast enough to put me at ease.

"Do you know how difficult it is to hold the same position for hours on end, my love?"

His deep blue eyes peered over his paintbrush, crinkled at the corners by a smile. "Of course, I do. About as difficult as standing and holding a paintbrush for hours on end."

We both laughed. I continued my duty as his muse, by holding perfectly still.

"Please, let's take a break soon," I said, knowing that soon the light would be too bad for him to see.

"Almost, I just want to finish up those obsidian eyes. Then we will quit for the day."

I was supposed to be staring off into the distance. I couldn't help but keep my eyes on him. Twenty-four years is not a long time to live, when the years are happy and placid. Sadly, those years of my life had been emotionally cruel, lonely. This man, squinting at his canvas, with a strong body as straight as an arrow, had changed my future in the course of a single three-day adventure. The adventure had bloomed into something beautiful, bringing us to where we were now. Life's bleakness had given way to light and love.

"Alright, I suppose I'll go blind if I don't stop now." He said, dropping his brush in a jar of turpentine.

"Thank goodness." I collapsed backward on the damask chaise in mock exhaustion. Julien walked toward me, wiping his hands on a bit of cloth. "The lady has had enough for today, or has she?"

I knew that look in his eye, I often had the same look for him. "Not here, someone could come in."

"No one has ever bothered us here," he said, moving on top of me, pressing his mouth against mine.

I let myself indulge in a long, slow kiss, then nipped at his bottom lip. "Do that again, later."

"Yes, my lady." He nipped my lip back, pulling me up with him.

"I shall wash and see you at dinner."

"Be on time, I have news," I said.

"News?" he looked apprehensive.

"Just go. I promise, it's good." I pushed him toward the door.

After dinner, he took the news beautifully. I was afraid the thought of an added burden would make him nervous. Much to my relief, Julien didn't see it that way, at all.

"My darling." He kissed my hand, holding me to him. "We will be well away, safe in a home of our own when your time is near. Are you afraid, at all?"

He continued to hold me, his breath skimming the back of my neck.

"I was at first, but not now. Everything will be wonderful, will it not?"

"Indeed, it will. Everything will be wonderful."

"Still with me? Want that water yet?" I pause for Jack, but he shakes his head.

"I'm still with you. Be prepared to answer some questions when you've finished."

"I'll answer whatever you ask." I continue.

"My pregnancy did nothing to speed up our time line. Our plan had been to leave when the portrait was finished, and it was almost upon us. I tried to get Julien to leave many times, but he refused to leave until the portrait was completed, and on its way to his own master. He was adamant he finish his masterpiece, making sure it was in safe hands. His need kept us in danger longer, but Julien could not be convinced to abandon the project.

The final week was torture for me. I feared for my husband's return every moment of every day. When Julien told me the portrait was finished, a huge weight lifted. This meant as soon as the painting was dry and sent off, we could make our escape.

Julien led me into the warm, sunny conservatory that had been our home for these many, precious weeks. We stopped next to the yellow, damask chaise, which had served as my seat for the portrait. Taking my hand, Julien pressed my fingertips to his lips and then turning it over, kissed my palm and the inside of my wrist.

"Darling, the end of the portrait, is the true beginning for us. It will be hard, you will no longer be a Marchioness of France, but how else could we possibly live?"

"I've no regrets. I would leave this life for you again, and again. For it is no life without you."

Julien told me to close my eyes, then sweetly led me to face the portrait. He stood close behind me, with his hands on my waist.

"Open your eyes," he whispered.

I was amazed. Julien had created a stunning work of art. Masterful brushstrokes, intricate details, everything was perfection. The portrait looked fully dimensional, as if I could step off the canvas and into the room. My face had been painted with such loving care, it appeared to me as if I was gazing at my reflection. He painted me as he first saw me--Aphrodite wrapped in white.

"It's magnificent. You have outdone yourself."

"You are an easy subject to paint, my love. I am truly grieved that we cannot take it with us."

I felt the atmosphere in the room change, when I heard a familiar voice say, "What a touching scene."

My blood ran cold. Instantly, I felt an icy sweat creep down my back. Julien, instead of releasing me, tightened his grip on my waist.

"Don't be afraid." he whispered.

But, I was afraid. Afraid as I had never been in my life. We had been deeply foolish, idle even, now there would be a price to pay. Laughable, it *seems to me now, how we thought we could remain as long as we did, then escape without a trace. But I knew so little of the world then.*

I stepped out of Julien's grasp, my head held high. I turned to face Charles.

"Charles," I began to speak, but he didn't let me get far.

He held up his hand, for a terrifying moment, I thought he was going to laugh. But, the half-smile turned into an ugly sneer and I shuddered.

"Don't speak to me, please don't try to explain this away. I have had it from the servants, how you visit his room every night. This is my home, everyone in it belongs to me. Did you think you could get away with this? You are nothing better than a whore."

Julien moved along side of me.

"She is no whore, just as you are no husband."

I wanted to scream, I wanted to cry, I wanted to grab Julien and run. I could plainly see what was happening, there would be no escape for either of us. Charles would challenge Julien, and I would be lost. I could see no way out.

Charles pointed his finger at the man I loved, as four men, all friends of Charles, entered the room. "Lock him in the cellar. I will deal with him, later."

Julien tried to fight them, but there was no use. As they were dragging him out, he shouted, "Don't give up, Millicent!"

Life can change in an instant, when you least expect it. The tears flowed. I squeezed my eyes shut, trying to think. Charles slapped me so hard I was driven to the ground. Because that wasn't good enough, I also received a swift kick in the belly, dealt by his pointed leather boot. I was sobbing, in unbelievable pain.

"I was a good husband to you. I provided you a fortune and I never hurt you. You not only failed in your duty to give me an heir, you whored yourself out at the first opportunity. You have shamed me. No one will have any sympathy for you."

Charles grabbed my arms and hauled me, painfully to my rooms. Once inside, he flung me on the bed. I had never seen him violent, only indifferent. I was terrified of what he might do next.

"Pack your things. Only the plainest, most modest things you own. No jewels. You won't need them in the convent."

"Charles, what will you do with him?"

He turned around. I flinched, thinking he would hit me, again.

Instead, he spit out, "What do you think?" and left me.

I was wracked with intense cramping, when the bleeding began. I knew I had lost the baby, delicate inside me. I removed my gown and sat in the bathtub, sobbing heavily, hoping for the pain to be over quickly. It was so new, only a few weeks. Everything had been for naught. I should have known a woman couldn't make her own destiny, not in this world. All I truly cared for was Julien. How could I possibly save us both? My heart was broken for my love, for the loss of our child.

I laid there in a daze. I began to think on my dreams of Jupiter. More often of late, he had shown me the way to the little cottage, deep in the woods. He told me, if I ever found myself in distress, I was to seek him out. But, this was surely nonsense, only dreams. I was grasping at fairy tales, a girlish fantasy.

And then, very surely, I knew it was not. He was real. And he was waiting for me, just where he said he'd be. The bag of tea was always there, always full. I took it for granted the little cloth bag would always be in the compartment of my jewelry case. Jupiter was clearly able to play with one's mind. I just had to hope he was powerful in other ways, as well.

Carefully, I cleaned myself and dressed, throwing on a black cape. There was still blood, but it was light enough, like my monthly cycle. The pain was more intense, but I could not be bothered with it. If I didn't act, I would lose Julien, too. There was no time to waste, but it would be difficult to sneak out of the chateau.

Surprisingly, there was no one outside my door. Charles must have thought I lacked the courage to try an escape. I made my way as silently as I could through the unlit hallways. Still, not seeing a soul. Bracing myself, I walked down the grand, front staircase, every step a jolt to my sore body. It took me more than thirty minutes to make my way through the chateau to the outside, finally able to breathe in fresh air.

Once my foot hit gravel, I ran. As if our lives depended on it, and they did.

When I reached the edge of the woods, I stopped and turned around for one last look at my home. What I didn't know was I would never again look on that hated place with mortal eyes. I followed the path shown to me in my dreams. Everything was familiar, and I made my way easily. After walking for hours, and who knows how many miles, the sun began to set. Cold panic made its way around my belly, but thankfully not for long.

The little cottage was the exact copy of the one from my dreams. Again, I didn't feel this was strange, I did not feel unnerved in any way. I felt only as if I was walking a path I was always meant too.

The wooden door creaked open, there was Jupiter. Just as I knew him, from my dreams. He was dressed like a peasant in a white shirt and linen trousers, the color of sand. This was no peasant I had ever seen. This was a Roman god, indeed. His power was evident, and I smiled through my tears, because I needed that power. He opened his arms to me. I ran into them, like a child.

"Please help me," I said.

"Hush now, dear one," his voice was deep, thunderous. "All will be well."

Jupiter took me into the cozy, little room, seating me by the fire. He put a glass of warm liquid into my hands.

"My name is actually Alexandre, Millicent," he said, as if he had read my mind, all of this still felt very natural to me.

"I have so much to ask," I said.

"Drink down that cup and you will have all the answers you need."

I didn't question him. I did as I was bid, I drained my cup dry. Instantly, all physical pain left me, I felt a dreamy, sleepiness take over. I could see everything. I saw Alexandre at my wedding, dancing endlessly, dressed as a prince. This is where Alexandre saw me for the first time and was taken with me. He felt a protectiveness for a sweet, innocent, and unhappy girl. After that night, he lived in this tiny cottage, so he could be close to me, in case I needed him.

Feeling my unhappiness, he visited me in my dreams, attempting to offer some cheer, some solace, and some hope for the future. He waited for me, biding his time. There was nothing malicious or frightening. Nothing to scare me, simply a need to protect, to watch over. I then saw he wasn't human. He woke only at night, drinking blood to sustain himself. I shuddered when I witnessed him draining a woman, now dead in his arms.

"Are you going to do the same to me?" I asked, dreamily.

"No, never. I saw something in you, Millicent. Something worth preserving. My hope has always been one day, when you are ready, you will join me as a companion. We can be a family."

"I can't. I could never take a life. I've come here to ask your help to save my love. Surely, you know all that has happened."

He looked down, I could see that he was measuring his words, carefully.

"I know why you have come, and I will help you."

I felt such relief, a renewed energy helped me sit up straight in my chair.

"However, I want something from you in return."

All I could think was, of course he does. All men are selfish when you come down to it. "You want me to become what you are." I knew the answer.

"Yes, but I will give you time. I will save your lover, and then I will give you five years with him."

"Five years!" I didn't mean to shout, but I did.

"Would you like five years to live in happiness with the man you love, or would you like none? You have to give something, in order to receive something. This is the way of the world."

He was threatening me, giving me an ultimatum, which seemed incongruous to what he had shown me. But, I was desperate. In my desperation, I thought to agree, then once Julien was free, he and I would escape.

"I agree."

He smiled, and said, "I knew you were a smart girl. Trust me, Millicent. I only want what is best for you. Everything will work out as it should."

I nodded. Hope sprang to my chest.

"You will remain here. I will go to the chateau, rescue Julien and bring him to you. The two of you will then be free to go."

"I should come. Even after what's happened, I don't want anyone killed."

"You will only slow me down. No harm will come to anyone inside the chateau. Stay here, please, and wait for our return."

I reluctantly agreed. If what he showed me was true, Alexandre was fast, strong. He was right, I would only slow him down and be in the way.

"Hurry, I fear they have killed him already."

Without another word, Alexandre was gone.

Time seemed to drag slower than ever before. In reality, it was only about an hour, before I heard movement outside. Alexandre burst through the door, covered in blood. He was alone. I sank to my knees.

"I am so sorry, I was too late," I heard him say, right before the world went black.

I woke, remembering fully, everything that had happened. I lay on a soft bed, with Alexandre seated on a chair next to me.

"Tell me." I could barely choke out the words.

"They had killed him before I arrived, shot in the head. They were searching the grounds for you, with torches. I'm sorry, but I killed Charles, and his friends. Your servants were untouched."

"I'm glad. They had it coming." Never would I have thought I would say such words, but the night had changed me. My heart was hard.

"I'll join you," I said. "But I must return to the chateau, once more."

Quickly, Alexandre explained to me what he would do, how it would feel. I cared about nothing. He worked the majick right there on the bed. When his fangs pierced my throat, I had a change of heart, feeling I would rather die. But, Alexandre worked his trick too quickly, it was too late to alter my course.

105

Alexandre explained to me later that he calls this point of no return, deepest midnight. Panic is felt, along with a desire to turn back, but at that point there is no turning around. It felt like dying, at first. And then, when it was over, I felt more alive than I ever had before. My senses were clearer, more sharply focused. Unfortunately, this also meant my feelings were deeper and more keenly felt. I knew it was going to be a long eternity, and for me, deepest midnight would never end.

The next evening, my first as an immortal, I returned to the abandoned chateau. Alexandre waited outside, in a cart pulled by two beautiful black horses, pilfered from my stables. His job was to carefully take the still wet portrait and place it in the stone cabin, where it would be left to wait for us. While Alexandre performed this task for me, I packed my jewels, including Marie Antoinette's sapphire bracelet, a few pieces of art, and any gold I could find. I was going to need money for the centuries. I never went into the cellar.

Then I torched the place."

CHAPTER SEVENTEEN

"I still wear the gold band on my left hand. It's a part of me now, I never take it off." I pause, wondering how to finish, "The rest isn't all that important. Not in regard to our current situation, anyway."

Perched on the chest at the foot of my bed, I look toward Jack. With my long story concluded, I shut my mouth, waiting. Jack is silent for some time, sitting in the armchair by the mantle. When I can no longer bear the quiet, I decide to break it.

"Jack, what are you thinking? Your silence is killing me."

"I guess, I'm just having a hard time accepting all this. I'm really trying my best. It's just so unbelievable, isn't it? I mean, think about it from my perspective. But, it explains what you see in me. You think I'm what, Julien reincarnated?" he sounds slightly annoyed.

"I think you are, but really don't know, Jack. And maybe it doesn't even matter."

"It matters. Would you have wanted me if I had looked nothing like him? I wonder if you would have given me a second glance."

I'm a little taken aback, wondering if he missed the entire point of the story. I just bared my soul to him. The only people on the planet who fully know all of this, are Annie and Alexandre. I try not to be defensive.

"Of course, I would have. Okay, it's true I was initially attracted to you because of the resemblance. But, Jack, you're different. Your personality, I mean. I have fallen in love with you, with who *you* are." I try to convince him, but he appears unmoved by my plea.

"The fact remains, that you wouldn't have given me a shot had I not resembled your dead lover."

"Hold on. I can't believe you're angry. I just shared my very personal story with you, a story that, before you, was only known by a grand total of two people."

I can't believe his reaction, actually I am borderline offended.

Jack takes a deep breath, rubbing his eyes. "Look, I'm sorry. This sort of thing doesn't happen to me every day. My girlfriend is a vampire and I may be her reincarnated 18th century lover, who was murdered by her husband. Kind of a lot to take in. I love you, Millicent, I do. I've never felt anything like it."

"But," I prompt him. He just told me he loves me, shouldn't that be what we're focusing on?

"I guess the but is, I'm afraid you fell for me for the wrong reasons. And now that I really think about it, what kind of future can we have?"

"We can have any future we want. Have you not been paying attention?"

I'm getting mad and feel my neck heat up. Vampires can and do have very human reactions, sometimes.

"I'm so much older than you as it is. Physically, anyway." I narrow my eyes as he tries to explain his reasoning further. "I'm a thirty-eight-year-old man. By all appearances, you are a twenty-four-year-old woman. I'm going to go downhill quickly, while you remain as you are."

"One of the points of telling you this story, and revealing myself as immortal, is to lay out the possibility of you becoming immortal, too. I guess I didn't make that clear. I don't have to lose you, again."

The look on his face frightens me. *Oh, shit. I probably should have left out that last part.*

"You do think I'm Julien."

"I didn't mean to say that, really. You are Jack, your own unique person. What I meant was, I don't have to lose love, again."

Jack doesn't answer right away. He stands up with his hands on his hips and takes a turn around the room. This is another way in which Jack differs from Julien. Julien didn't need much time to gather his thoughts and measure his words, he just spoke.

"I need air." And with that, he's gone.

Jack couldn't bolt out of the house fast enough. Humans have no need for preternatural speed when faced with fight or flight.

I'm an idiot. What made me think he would accept anything I told him? Did I think he would just take it all in, say "Cool!", and flop on the bed to be drained of blood and filled back up again? Just like that? I guess I did. Disappointment floods my body.

When I walked to that stone cabin two centuries ago, it was as if I knew what I was walking toward. I felt no fear, I never questioned it. It felt like a natural progression of events from start to finish. Destiny. If Jack doesn't feel it, then maybe this wasn't his destiny. If I force immortality on him, he will hate me forever. I know I can't do that. He must choose for himself. Even if he doesn't choose a forever with me. And if I turn him, what will Alexandre do? I suspect he will forgive me, being generally all talk, but who knows?

With dawn only moments away, I don't have time to think. Going to bed thinking about a positive outcome is a sure way to make one come about, right? *Keep telling yourself that.*

Exhausted, I leave my clothes in a pile and slip into my bed.

I wake the next evening to no news. Checking my phone, I see not a single individual, mortal or immortal, has attempted to contact me. My heart is heavy at the realization Jack hasn't reached out at all. *Way to leave a girl hanging.*

A sharp knock at my door makes me jump about ten feet. Alexandre enters wearing an amused smile, I quickly drag my sheet up to my chin.

"A startled vampire. What's become of you, Mills?"

I am in no mood to banter. "What do you want, Alexandre. Come to gloat?"

"Oh, come now, Mills. I am sorry you are sad, genuinely. I won't tell you I told you so. Humans are inferior, very rarely does one come upon a mortal who can mentally handle all this. Trust me, it's better this way."

"Right, as you've said before."

"Think of our family. Annie and you were special. Uniquely suited to this existence. I have seen mistakes made. Mortals unable to handle the change for an eternity. You have to be very careful."

"Yes, I understand. I'd like to know some other facts, right now. The detectives showing up in the middle of the day, and James showing up with a gun, distracted me from talking to you about the note. Also, why do you keep disappearing?"

My sadness turns into boiling anger.

"I've simply been giving you your space to get over this obsession, once and for all. As to the warning and the note, they were not meant to be threatening, merely an urge to use caution. It is moot now, so we can just forget about it and move on."

"Forget it? The centuries must be making you as mad as a hatter. There is no way I will ever forget it. You should know me better, after all this time. Please, get out."

Even though I keep my voice even and don't yell, I know I sound murderous.

Alexandre blankly looks at me for a minute, then gets up and moves away.

Before opening the door, he says with his back still turned, "Don't forget who helped you that fateful night, and who has done nothing but love and shelter you, ever since. You've never been easy to live with, Mills."

No kidding. I have suffered through long bouts of melancholy, bleak periods when I was nothing but a storm cloud. They suffered along with me. However, I have also experienced moments of joy. During those times I've been almost fun, I'm sure of it. I know at least Annie would agree, and right now, that's all I care about.

Leaving my room, I hear Alexandre in his, actually singing to himself. Something occurs to me. Alexandre has always been at his highest when I'm at my lowest. Thinking back through the endless years, the truth sits like lead in my stomach.

When I am happy, when I have a lover, and when I am enjoying myself, he is the miserable one. It's also when I'm sad, lower than low, I spend the most time with Alexandre, occasionally accepting him as a lover. Shortly after he changed me, we were lovers for maybe fifty years. I was in such pain then, feeling my only opportunity for real love had come and gone. I craved the companionship of a man, which Alexandre provided. He doted on me. It didn't hurt that physically, the man resembled Poseidon, and was not only god of the sea, but god of the sack.

He was a wonderful distraction. I didn't love him in a romantic way, nor did he speak to me of romantic love. Part of me wonders if Annie was right. Had Alexandre loved me all this time? It's more likely he simply sees me as his creation, his eternal doll, as if possessive of a beloved toy.

Whatever the reason, I am not going to play games with him. Perhaps it's time I move on from Alexandre, out of his shadow I have comfortably hidden in for so long. There's no reason why I cannot make it on my own.

However, the prospect of another two and a half centuries alone is daunting.

CLARA WINTER

CHAPTER EIGHTEEN

I'm edging closer to the idea of striking out on my own, at least for a while. Annie's the only one welcome to join me, at this moment, and I'm sure she would. Feeling the need to break more than one pattern tonight, I dig out a black pencil skirt to go with my sky high, black Mary Jane's, and silky, black t-shirt. I leave my hair down, then head out into the jungle-like heat of this Savannah night.

I'm greeted on the street by the usual sounds of cars, mixed with people laughing and talking in Forsyth Park. The creamy white gardenias are in bloom. The sweet fragrance follows me down the sidewalk. The news vans moved on, the media being a fickle beast. Deciding the soft sounds of the fountain would be heavenly, I walk into the park, finding a nearby bench.

There are a few tourists dotted around. I people watch for a bit. After a few minutes of trying to guess where people are from, I hear a familiar voice, not far away. A voice which makes me cringe. Turning my head, I see Timothy Woods, the movie star. He's chatting with a very young, very gorgeous woman. I should say he is chatting at her, because he doesn't stop to take a breath for a full five minutes. I can't hear what he's saying, but I'm sure he is the star of his story. He doesn't seem at all sad, given recent events.

Finally, it seems he has exhausted his lung capacity and shuts up. The woman is smiling ear-to-ear, clearly star struck. Poor thing. Before I know it, he has her pushed against the gate surrounding the fountain and gropes her in a very inappropriate manner. My blood boils, but I stay where I am, waiting for her reaction. It's negative. I clearly hear her say, "You hurt me," as she tries to push him back.

I'm up in a heartbeat, walking over, trying to keep my preternatural speed under control. It sounds like he's trying to talk her into something, because I hear him say, "Come on," twice.

"Timothy," I say, loud and clear.

He immediately backs up, sticking his hands in his pockets, looking my way. His megawatt smile loses its strength by about fifty percent.

When I stop, just in front of them, he weakly says, "Hey…you."

"You don't remember me? We just met."

"Of course, I remember you. You're the chick who lives in that big house over there," he says, pointing in the wrong direction, but at least he's looking me in the eye, this time.

"Yep, I'm that chick. It's Millicent."

"I know, I know. How are you, tonight?"

"Oh, I'm great. How are you and your friend?"

I turn toward the woman who is pretty clearly looking for an exit, her eyes are darting all over the park.

"We're great," says Timothy.

"Are you great?" I ask the woman.

"No, not really," she answers.

"Let's get you a ride home." I pull out my phone.

"I don't think that's necessary, I can get her home," offers Timothy.

"That's not happening. Besides, I'm all done. Your ride should be pulling up right over there in about two minutes. On me," I say, then gesture toward the southwest corner of the park.

"Thank you, really," she says, without so much as a glance toward Timothy.

Timothy lets out an annoyed sigh, after she walks away, "Why did you do that? We were fine."

"She was most definitely, not fine. I don't like bullies, and I especially don't like men who prey on women."

"What? Please, I'm no predator." He leans against the gate.

"Right, and I'm short," I pause, interested in something else. "How are you doing with the loss of your friend?"

"Kathryn? Fine, we weren't really friends. Just coworkers, I guess." He shrugs his shoulders.

"Most human beings would still be upset over the loss of a coworker," I point out, my hands on my hips.

"Sure. I'm sad, of course. Kathryn was hot, total waste."

I itch to take this guy out, pure scumbag. Once again, his eyes roam all over my body.

"What are you doing, tonight?"

"I'm busy. But, I have a feeling you'll be seeing me again, sooner than you think."

"Ok, that's a funny thing to say. How's your friend, the one with the big...smile?"

If he hadn't had the sense to change the course of that question, I would have laid him out, right here. Witnesses be damned.

"Timothy, you are one disgusting waste of space."

I turn on my heel, walking back toward home. Timothy yells an expletive at me. I don't bother to turn around. Get it all out of your system now, I think, your days are numbered. If my encounter with this jerk has given me anything, it's another name for my suspect list. Not that I'm really making a list, or investigating, but it would be nice if the police found Kathryn's killer. The spotlight would be lifted from my family, and the killer would be behind bars, unable to hurt anyone again.

I come to a stop in front of my house, considering something. Could I find the killer if I opened myself up and looked around? This is how I find the majority of my meals.

I can sense an unclean soul, but I can't see what they've actually done until I'm drinking from them. I figure it can't hurt to try, so I stand there on the sidewalk in the light from the streetlamp. I close my eyes, opening myself up to evil. After a few minutes, I close up the floodgates. It's not working. This only serves as a reminder that there are a lot of nasty people out there. I feel sad, disoriented for a moment, before reminding myself the good in the world really does outweigh the bad.

"What are you doing? Have you gone catatonic?" Annie's bright voice calls down from the porch.

Laughing, I say, "No, I was trying something. It didn't work."

We stay outside, sitting in our much-loved rocking chairs.

"I met our favorite film star in the park, a few minutes ago."

"Is it the guy who couldn't stop staring at my breasts?" Annie rocks, one leg crossed over the other.

"The very same. He was assaulting a woman."

She abruptly stops rocking. "Tell me you ripped out his beating heart and ate it?"

"Oh, I plan to. Want to join me?" Annie starts to get up, but I put out my hand to halt her. "Not right now. Believe me, it was hard to hold back, but I think it's best if we wait until he's out of Savannah. I was thinking we should visit him at his home, one night soon."

Annie grunts in disappointment and resumes her seat. "I guess you're right. *Fine*. What were you doing on the sidewalk just now?"

I tell her of my idea to try to find Kathryn's killer.

"But, it didn't work. I was actually thinking Timothy would make a good suspect, but I can't know unless I drink from him."

"So, why didn't you? Hello?" She taps her head.

"I can't believe I didn't think to do that. I blame it on being distracted." I start tapping my foot, then stop, thinking of Jack.

"We still can, come on." Annie takes off down the porch steps and I follow, hot on her heels.

"I hope he's still there," I say to the back of her head.

"He can't have gone far, we'll find him."

I'm very adept at running in my stilettos. In no time, we are in the park, nearing the fountain. He's not there. Annie jogs around the water feature, as I scan the surrounding area.

"There!" I shout, pointing to the entrance of the park. "He's getting into a car."

"You stay here, I got this," Annie says.

A couple of people in the park are watching us like we're crazy. I move out of the way behind a tree, so Timothy, and these tourists, can't see me. After a couple of minutes, I hear Annie's laughter, much softer than usual. She's trying to keep a low profile. She walks with Timothy, then pushes his back into the same tree I'm hiding behind. They are just out of view from the handful of people around the fountain.

"Hey there, gently," he says. I want to puke.

"Mills, come here," Annie whispers.

I walk around to where she has Timothy mesmerized, leaning against the tree trunk.

"Let me do it," I say, right before sinking my teeth into his flesh. I drink for as long as it takes to see what's inside this guy's head.

When I finish, I step back and say, "Unclean soul, but not a murderer. We'll deal with him soon enough."

Annie knees him in the groin, leaving him crumpled in a heap at the base of the tree.

"He'll feel that when he wakes up," she says, throwing me a high five.

"Do you think we know enough about Alexandre and what we are?" I muse on the way home.

"I feel like I know enough, although I wonder if there is more to us. I know relatively little about Alexandre, considering."

"I know nothing about his history, before me. Whenever I ask, he just brushes me off with some non-committal answer, or another," I say.

"Me, too. I've always been curious, though. I wonder if something awful happened in his past, and he just doesn't care to relive it."

"Possibly. It would be nice to at least know what his origin is. Where is he from, who made him, and is that vampire still living? I don't see why it's so hard to talk about."

"Maybe for him, it is. Where do you think he's from?" Annie asks.

"When he first came to me in my dreams, I thought of him as the Roman God, Jupiter. Now and then, I refer to him as Poseidon. My feeling has always been Alexandre is either Ancient Greek or Roman."

"Definitely, Roman," decides Annie. "He has that Caesar look and bearing."

"Oh, god. Do not call him Caesar to his face. It's bad enough that he gets the Jupiter and Poseidon thing from me. His ego is inflated enough."

We both have a laugh, at the expense of our maker.

"I guess it is strange that we know nothing about his life pre-Millicent. I haven't known many other immortals, but now that I think about it, I'm pretty sure they're origins were not a secret.

Makes me think he's hiding something, but what?" wonders Annie.

"My thoughts, exactly. On the other hand, nothing has come back to haunt him in the two hundred forty plus years I've been with him."

"Am I awful, because I've never been too interested?" asks Annie.

"No, you've always had your own things going on. I have been with Alexandre almost non-stop, I should know more. Whenever I have asked him a question about his past, he brushes me off, and I just let it go. Maybe I should have been more insistent."

"I've been telling you to be more insistent for how long?"

"Oh, I don't know. *Forever.*" I give my friend a playful push.

"He's been so odd, lately. I hope we can all weather this storm," I add.

"Only time will tell, my friend," says Annie.

"No truer words were ever spoken."

"By the way, with all this stuff going on, I've forgotten to ask how things are with Jack. Anything new?"

"You could say there have been new developments...I told him everything. Everything about what I am, and everything about my past. Good call on the arm cutting idea, worked like a charm."

Annie pulls me to a stop, her mouth gaping open. "And? I can't believe it. What did he do?"

"He freaked out and bolted. Haven't heard from him since."

"Oh, Mills. I'm sorry. Just give him some time, he'll come around. How could he not?"

"Like you said before, only time will tell."

CHAPTER NINETEEN

Idleness isn't going to be my thing. I want to know more about what is going on. Is Jack the reincarnation of Julien, or is it some crazy coincidence? Were we meant to find each other again, or does this mean absolutely nothing? I'm going to do some more research in an effort to find out.

Resisting the temptation to click on what I'm sure are scientifically based quizzes, I delve deeper. Very quickly, I am rewarded with some articles of actual substance. The digital world still amazes me. The ease of accessing a universe of information is an incredible human achievement.

Alexandre may feel derisive toward mortals, but I am continually amazed by the innovations I've witnessed. Creativity abounds in mortal creatures. Perhaps it's the fact that a mortal feels their mortality, wishing to leave a lasting impression on the earth. It's a beautiful thing. For the most part, the immortals I have known are lackadaisical and decadent. With all the time in the world, what's the rush?

Well, for the first time in two hundred plus years, I'm compelled to rush. Time presses down on me. I can't deny that Jack is vulnerable. I'm terrified something could happen to him, even if he has decided he doesn't want me.

My deeper search uncovers an article which catches my eye. It has to do with something called karmic groups. Karmic groups are reincarnated souls who tend to be attracted to the same souls, over and over again. I love the idea of souls who have loved each other, coming together, time and again. But, what happens if you are stuck with a soul you can't stand, someone mean or evil? Does this mean you are destined to run into this soul, endlessly?

It doesn't sound very appealing. If I lose this version of Julien, will he find me again in another two hundred years? One thing is clear—although you may be pre-destined to be reunited with the love of your life, free will reigns. Choices can still be made which make it impossible to be together.

Is it important to know if Jack is the reincarnation of Julien? I don't think it will matter if he chooses to walk away from what we have. People walk away from real love all the time.

A person who wants to find out about their past lives can have a past life regression. I found some information on something called the Akashic Record. From what I understand, the Akashic Records are a collection of everything that has ever occurred in all of human history, including; feelings, thoughts, actions, and so much more. An individual can access these records through a soul reading, performed by someone who has been specially trained in this technique. Or with practice, an individual can learn to access the records by themselves. Of course, there is no scientific evidence to back any of these ideas up, but vampirism is not exactly a proven scientific fact, either. Yet, here I sit.

Coming across an article on innate talent, I click and scroll down. The article states a creative soul is often creative in all incarnations of life. This is interesting to me. Julien was a talented, accomplished painter, while Jack is an actor and writer. All creative fields.

I shut down my tablet and return it to the dark recesses of my nightstand. Just to torture myself, I check my phone again. Still no messages or texts. I could be really lame and call someone, just to make sure the phone is in good working order. The only thing that will do is make me feel worse. I'm not a lovesick teenager. I'm a grown ass, immortal woman.

This house feels like a prison I need to break free of. I'm not feeling merciful, tonight. Taking a few unknowing drops from some unsuspecting fool isn't going to slake my furious hunger. What I held back from telling Jack was, every now and then, we do take a life. I was telling the truth when I said we spare the innocent from death. Accidents will happen, especially when one is newly changed. But, by and large, we are respectful of life.

Once in a while, an occasion calls for draining an entire body. When nothing but gorging will do, we are careful to select a mortal whose soul is unclean. In short, murderers and rapists. Unfortunately, the world teems with such individuals.

Sitting in my room, I close my eyes, opening myself up. Almost immediately, I feel the evil calling to me. If this is not a wakeup call to mankind, I don't know what is. It shouldn't be so easy. I don't even bother to slip on shoes. My ruthless animal won't even know what hit him, let alone have time to take in my appearance. I walk up to the attic, then step out onto the roof. I swiftly make my way over the rooftops, until I am right above him.

He is slinking in an alleyway, stalking his next victim like prey. I see the pretty redhead he watches through the kitchen window. She is busily preparing herself something to eat. I close my mind to him. Seeing what he has done and what he has planned for this young woman will ruin my appetite.

With his back to me, I work quickly. One hand goes over his mouth as the other slips around his stomach. In one swift motion, I pull him against me, sinking my lengthened canines into the soft, sweaty flesh at his throat. Not yummy, but when I taste the hot, thick blood, I don't notice his grime. He doesn't fight, most don't. I'm not sure what it is about a vampire's fangs, but they seem to incapacitate quickly.

I drain this foul creature dry in record time and take him back to the rooftops with me. You can't just leave a body in an alley. That is sloppy. After all, it's only polite to clean up after yourself. The cleanup is another, more practical reason why we prefer to take small drinks from the innocent. Innocents taste better. Being pure, their blood is sweeter. A human with an unclean soul has more of a bitter taste, but like I said, sometimes you just need *all* the blood.

It is not easy to dispose of a body, I don't care what you think you've learned from crime shows. Doing so, has only become more difficult with time. My go to method, taught by Alexandre, is to find a freshly dug pit at the cemetery. You find yourself a plot that has been dug out to accept its new occupant the next day. Dig down a few more feet, drop in your body, cover it, and there you go. Once the dearly departed has been lowered, buried over your evil corpse, he will be hidden forever. Evil corpses are almost always male. *Go figure.*

I'm lucky tonight as there are two plots ready. Using my hands, preternatural strength, and speed, I take care of my chore. Crawling out of the pit, I can only imagine what I look like. If Jack thinks becoming an immortal isn't for him, he should see me now. He won't need any more convincing. Without delay, I begin my dance back home over the rooftops.

I need the type of scrub down they give you after a nuclear reactor leak. Hopping onto the roof of the house next door to mine, I feel him. Jack is there. For the love of all that's holy, his timing couldn't be worse. I literally look like I just crawled out of a grave, and probably smell like it, too.

Peering down I see him talking with Annie, on the porch. She knows I'm up here. I have no doubt she placed herself in the exact spot she is in, so his back would be turned on me. Not wasting this opportune moment, I noiselessly slip into the house using the same attic window I left from. I tear into my room, stripping the clothes from my body. Jumping into the shower, I wash in record time. Annie comes in as I'm stepping out onto the bathmat.

"Well, you know he's here. I tried to kill as much time as I could. He wants to come up, so just throw on your robe, and I'll burn these." She picks up my clothes, keeping them at arm's length.

I don't even have time to give her my thanks. She's out the door and moments later, I can hear Jack in the bedroom. I guess this must be it, he has come to tell me his decision. He's made me wait, so he can wait a few more minutes for me. I apply some French lavender body lotion, comb out my hair, and select my favorite black silk robe. No need to make this too easy for him.

When I've done all I feel like doing, I know it's time to face the music. He hasn't tried to talk to me through the door, so it must be bad news. I am suddenly very angry with him, or maybe with myself. He must not feel for me what Julien did, or it wouldn't be so easy for him to walk away. *Let's just get this over with.*

CHAPTER TWENTY

Steeling myself, I open the door, then walk into the bedroom. Jack is standing in front of the mantle, gazing at the portrait, with his hands in the pockets of what I can't help but notice is a pair of sexy, form fitting jeans. I always keep the portrait covered, so he must have pulled back the curtains. He looks so good that it's all I can do to keep from jumping him right there on the area rug.

I sit on the edge of the bed, wanting him more than I can almost bear. Keeping his eyes on the floor, he turns away from the portrait, and walks around to where I'm sitting. In a movement that speaks volumes, he dips down, takes my face in his hands, and kisses me.

I'm so unprepared, that if I had any breath, he would have taken it away. This is not a goodbye kiss. This is a kiss that speaks of beginnings. All my anger melts. I feel as if I could cry. There is a telltale lump in my throat as I kiss the man I love with all my soul.

Jack pulls me up to my feet, "Millicent, I worship and adore you. I've never known anyone like you, and never will. Please forgive me for being such a fool. It was unfair of me to leave you hanging. This is a big deal, a life changing decision, I just had to be sure."

"A life changing decision. Does this mean you've decided to join me, *truly join me?*"

"Yes, but not yet. I must take care of some things first, tie up my life, the best way that I can. And, first things first."

Jack unties my robe and his left-hand moves around my bare waist, pulling me toward him. With his right hand, he gently bends my head to the side and begins kissing my neck, right below my ear. I'm so mad for him, I can't wait. I throw my arms back, letting the robe fall to the ground, and push him onto the bed.

Pulling his t-shirt off, over his head, he laughs, "Impatient, much?"

"Much," I say, playfully, as I tug off his pants.

He is ready for me, and I am on fire for him. Jack sits up on his elbows as I straddle him, impaling myself on his rigid penis. We moan together. Our mouths meet, as I begin to ride. With one hand behind my head and one on my back, Jack spins us around so that he is on top.

"Always so fast for you," he murmurs in my ear, making me giggle.

He's right. I typically feel such an urgency to have him, I don't let myself savor the sensations. I wrap my legs around his, cradling him with my body, letting him take his time. As much as I try to hold back, it doesn't take us long. I reach climax, right before he does.

Jack is exhausted from working long days on set, coupled with sleepless nights with me. Before he drops off to sleep, I give him the rundown about what I learned from my very brief stint as researcher. He is interested by the idea of karmic groups.

"So, you're always tied to the people you love, that's a very comforting thought," he muses, and I agree.

"Is it important for you to know, Millicent? Really know, if I'm him?"

I don't even hesitate. "No, it's not important. Whether you are the same soul or not, makes no difference. You're stuck with me."

"Works for me," he pauses, "I just thought of something."

"Yes?"

"Are you actually letting me sleep over?"

I kiss the tip of his nose. "I guess, I am. But, don't make a big deal of it, or I'll make you go home."

We get all snuggly, with Jack's arms around me, and my cheek on his chest. After he falls asleep, I slip out of his grasp.

This may be the time for Jack to sleep, but I'm still in the middle of my waking hours. I smile when I realize that soon we will be on the same schedule.

And just like that, my happiness disappears. I can feel Alexandre in the house, and I feel his anger. Deciding the robe is too revealing, I throw on some pink sweats. Carefully, I close my mind to my maker. This is not something I do often, as I have never had cause, and it is hard. He is pacing in the living room. I know he is waiting for me, and this will be ugly. Where did Annie run off to? I would feel much better if she were here to act as a mediator.

When I'm standing in the living room, it's easy to see how tense Alexandre is. He is about to explode. He stands in the center of the room, head bowed, eyes closed, hands clasped behind his back, a vein bulging out of his forehead. He looks disheveled. His jeans and sweater are filthy, his hair is a mess. I wonder if he's been sleeping underground. I want to remark on his appearance, but for some reason, I hold back.

I say simply, in a quiet voice, "Alexandre."

He doesn't answer me, he doesn't look up. He appears to be working his hands together, behind his back. I suddenly have the feeling he is trying to keep himself from strangling me.

It's hard to explain everything I'm feeling in this moment. This is a man who has done nothing but protect me, care for me, for over two centuries. I have never had reason to fear him, yet I fear him now. My fear runs to Jack, sleeping helplessly upstairs. My strength is significant, but I have never tested it against Alexandre's. It seems clear to me that on my own, against him, I would lose.

As I'm running through all my options, which are pretty much nil, Alexandre finally raises his head, opening his eyes. My options being scarce, I decide to try and keep it light, turn on the charm. It may sound stupid, but it's all I've got. It has never been difficult for me to charm Alexandre. But then again, I've never been so frightened around him. I will have to put on my own performance and had better make it a good one. Trying to affect a face full of concern, I try again.

"Alexandre, are you ok? I'm so worried about you." Clasping my hands in front of me, like a sweet nun, I take a step toward him.

"Stop and sit." Alexandre points to the sofa, his eyes are hard, frightening.

"Of course, come sit next to me." It's all I can do to keep my voice clear, so he can't see my fear.

Sitting, I pat the cushion next to me. Alexandre ignores me, continuing to stand. He now has me in an even greater position of weakness. He fixes me in his fiery gaze.

"I will speak, you will listen. I've had enough, and it ends tonight."

I want to ask him what he's had enough of, and what does he think will end tonight, but my smart-assery will only make this situation worse. I can't help but think I am the only one of his children he seeks to control. He could care less where Annie is, or what she does. I bide my time and taking his advice, remain silent.

"240 years, Millicent. That is how long I have waited for you to get over your thoughtlessness. What other man would wait so long? Julien was weak. He couldn't save you. I saved you!" He points to himself, face red, eyes glowing. "I took you in that night, I went to the chateau. I single handedly annihilated that waste of skin you called a husband and his buffoonish friends. When I found Julien in the cellar, do you think he was trying to escape, trying to get to you, trying to find a way out? He was sitting in the corner, nursing a bloody nose! Weak and stupid!"

It takes me only a moment to process what I'm hearing, but then I know. I know what he is saying. My fear multiplies, but so does my anger.

"He was alive." My voice a whisper.

Alexandre's completely unfazed. "Yes, he was alive. The band of fools that included your husband were side-tracked by your disappearing act. I was not expecting a man like him to come along. Julien threw a wrench into everything, everything I had planned for us."

"Annie was right, then?" He knows what I'm really asking.

He nods his head. "Annie has always known my true feelings for you. I tried to seem ambivalent, but I've just been waiting for you to come to your senses. Waiting for you to see me as the hero, as you should have always seen me, waiting for you to love me in return."

DEEPEST MIDNIGHT

"Love you? I have loved you, Alexandre, just not in the way you wanted. To feel romantic love would be impossible, and more than you can understand. Right now, all I feel for you, is hate."

His face is like stone, and I know I've made a fatal mistake, but thoughts of charming this man are gone forever.

"I'm leaving. Jack is coming with me."

I start to get up and, in an instant, Alexandre is on top of me. His massive body, pressing me hard, into the sofa. I put my hands against his chest, and try to push him away, but I can't.

"It's gone too far for that, I'm afraid." He spits out the words in my face, "You're not going anywhere. If you think I'll let you leave with him, you're crazy." He grips my arms, shaking me violently.

"Alexandre, you're my friend and you're hurting me! You've ruined everything I've ever felt for you. I thought I could count on you, always." Blood tears spill from my eyes.
Alexandre freezes. His face changes. He puts his forehead on my chest, his arms around my waist, crying blood tears of his own. We lay in this awkward position for several minutes.

"I've really lost you, now." I hear the anguish in Alexandre's voice, but my heart doesn't soften toward him. What he has broken is irreparable, though I still have to think about Jack.

"Don't hurt Jack, Alexandre. Please, just let him be and we will see what time has in store for us." I know Jack's life depends on my convincing Alexandre that I could, maybe one day, forgive him. But none of this matters.

My body reflexively jumps when I hear Jack yell, "What the hell is going on?!"

He is running toward us, then everything seems to happen in slow motion. Alexandre pushes off me, grabs Jack, and bolts out the front door. I try to run after them, but they are already gone. "Don't hurt him, Alexandre!"

CLARA WINTER

CHAPTER TWENTY-ONE

Although Jack is a fit, rather tall man, he's no match for Alexandre. It's been an hour since the awful moment. Jack could be dead. I contacted Annie, and she's on her way. Luckily for me, Annie is more loyal to me than Alexandre.

I wandered around the streets, trying to guess where they may have gone, but to no avail, and I'm not surprised. If Alexandre doesn't want to be found, he won't be.

When Annie rushes through the door, I am in a state of utter panic. All thoughts of past lives and Julien, are gone. My thoughts are only of Jack. I can't lose him. Annie sits down, while I tell her what happened and what I learned. She is stunned into silence.

"I always knew he carried a torch for you, I thought that was a no-brainer. But, that he killed Julien, I just can't believe it. Mills, I'm so sorry. Surely, Jack...," she is trying to be tactful.

"I don't know. I think I would feel it if he were dead. Either that, or Alexandre would return and throw it in my face."

"I can't believe we are talking about the same Alexandre. This is crazy."

"I've never seen him like that, Annie. He was insane. But, maybe I was able to get through to him a little, by the end. He was crying and seemed broken."

"Woah. Don't hate me, but I almost feel a little bad for him." Annie bites her lip, looking down.

"For Alexandre? He's a murderer and a liar."

"I know, I know. What he did was unforgivable and sick, but it was done out of love."

"Let's just stick with unforgivable and sick. You don't do those things to someone you love."

Annie hugs me. We try to brainstorm how we can find Jack. I had, of course, attempted to call and text Alexandre, on the off chance he would answer. But, of course, he didn't.

We decide to split up, doing a good old-fashioned canvas of the neighborhood, assuming Alexandre is still nearby. It seems safe to assume he is in the area with two hours to go until sunrise.

Annie and I head out, although neither of us is optimistic. I am opening my thoughts to Alexandre, but Annie isn't. We decide to keep her involvement under wraps until we find them, thus retaining an element of surprise. Annie is the spy, more experienced in these scenarios than I am. So, with my mind calling out to my maker, I scour my agreed upon area.

As I begin to get more desperate, I beg and plead with him. I am broadcasting thoughts of friendship, love, forgiveness, and innocence. I actually have little faith he will do the right thing, but I will crumble if I lose hope completely in this mad situation.

The streets of historic Savannah are dead at four a.m. In my current mood, who knows what would happen to anyone getting in my way. It's hypocritical thinking since I am hoping against hope Alexandre will not take the innocent life of Jack but give me a break. It's been a rough night.

When we reach the end of our areas, Annie and I are supposed to meet up in the middle of Chippewa Square. I am the first to arrive, with a half hour until sunrise. Very soon thereafter, I spot Annie coming down Bull Street. She looks at me, purses her lips, and shakes her head, telling me everything I need to know.

This is it. It is over. Jack is dead, he must be. Why would Alexandre keep him alive and not contact me? I honestly feel numb. I know the grief will come and I will deal with it, but not right now. I simply cannot. I'm running on autopilot.

Annie takes my hand, without saying a word, we turn toward home. I probably shouldn't feel safe, returning to the home I shared with Alexandre, but I do, at least for now. He is a slave to the dawn as much as I am, and so, he will also be closing his eyes for the coming daylight hours.

We cut it close, just closing the door on the rising sun. For a moment, I have a thought to remain in the street, meeting the sun head on. I hesitate on the porch, looking behind me. Annie pulls me inside. "Don't you even think about it."

"Too late."

"That's the coward's way out, Mills. You are no coward. We will take on Alexandre, another day."

She says nothing about saving Jack. She's thinking the same thing I am. Jack is dead. Two loves with the same face, dead. What are the chances I will get a third shot? Probably, not stellar. Annie doesn't let go of my hand until we are in my room. She lets me go to pull back the covers, then gently pushes me in. I can smell Jack on the sheets, I want to get up, but the sun is rising, my eyelids fall. Annie covers me up, walks around to the other side of the bed then crawls in next to me. *Thank goodness for this woman, Miss Rebel.* I close my eyes, everything goes blissfully black.

When I wake, I'm a little startled because my face is wet. I wipe my hand across my face and look down at my red hands. I realize I have been crying tears of blood while I slept. I think about showering and changing, but then ask myself, why bother? Annie comes in with a glass full of blood, putting it in my hands. It's pleasantly warm.

"I got an order to go, drink up." She just can't help herself.

I do as I'm told, realizing I am just about dying of hunger. The glass is a large one, but I drain it in two gulps. Annie disappears into the bathroom, then comes back out with a damp washcloth. She wipes off my face like I'm a child.

"If you haven't noticed the bedding, most of it should be tossed." I look around me, it looks like someone has been stabbed to death in my bed.

"Jesus, Annie. I'm so sorry, I didn't realize."

"I know, no biggie. Go grab a shower, while I strip the sheets. We can talk about our next step when you get out."

It feels good to be told what to do. I don't care to make any decisions, so I'll gladly let Annie drive. She's good people, or vampire, or whatever the hell.

Showering holds no interest for me, so I opt to wash my face and change. By the time I step back into my bedroom, the crime scene of my bed has been disposed of, replaced with clean linen.

"Well, love, what now?" Annie asks, simply.

"He must be…," I stop, unable to finish.

"Yeah. We should leave Savannah. Any place you want to explore?"

"No, not particularly." I slump myself into the chair.

"Ok, I get to choose. If it ever does come to a fight, we will need to rest up for a while."

"Would you truly join me in a fight against Alexandre, Annie? He's your maker, too. It's asking a lot."

"I've never been particularly close with Alexandre, not like I have been with you. I was his consolation prize, after you went traipsing off for a while. I was always too independent, too rebellious for his taste."

"Yes, he likes them submissive, doesn't he? And, you've always suited my taste, just fine. You're amazing."

I smile at her, this woman who has been my companion, friend, sister, and ally. She is remarkable, I would gladly die beside her.

"Let's get the hell out of here," I say.

We pack quickly, only what we need, and the few items which are special to us. Marie Antoinette's bracelet, carefully wrapped, goes in the front, zippered pocket of my backpack. I take my portrait off the wall and set it against the fireplace. I stand back, regarding it. A large painting in a fragile, antique frame won't be easy to flee with. Do I need it, or even want it? This portrait has kept me tied to the past, tied to a yearning for an impossible love.

Julien is long gone, and this picture only incites a despairing sadness. Julien, although I will never forget him, has been replaced in my heart by Jack. Jack is, or was, his own unique, special self. He may now be gone, but he is the one I will carry in my heart until I am finished. There will be no one else, ever. I'm also ready to move on from who the woman in the portrait was. I don't want to know her, anymore. I won't be weak, and easily lead, any longer. I hang the portrait back in its place over the mantle and draw the curtains back over the face of a woman who is becoming a stranger to me.

Annie and I meet up in the living room, and I take one more look around.

"I have no idea if I'll ever be back. I'll miss Savannah, but not this house."

My love for this mysterious city will never end, but this house is as dead to me, as the past. Suddenly, my phone alerts me that I have a text, and it's from Alexandre.

CHAPTER TWENTY-TWO

I may be unable to have a heart attack, but what I do feel is a sick pit in my stomach.

"Alexandre." Annie already knows without a word from me, the text is from him.

"It says, 'Emmet Park'. Do you think he knows you're here, yet?"

"I don't know. I will try to keep myself masked, hidden out of sight. There is no way you are going alone. Even if I stay back a block or two, I'll be able to hear everything you're saying."

"I think I should go alone, Annie. I love and appreciate you more than I can express, but there is no reason for you to endanger yourself, please stay here. I've stood behind others for too long, it's time for me to stand up for myself."

"Great sentiment, but it's not happening. Alone, neither of us are a match for Alexandre, but together we may have a chance. This isn't my first fight. Something I learned long ago is you always stand with your brothers, or this case, sister. I'll have your back."

I look at my friend, and a million things come to mind I should say. Instead, all I manage is, "Thanks," which seems paltry. She laughs, takes my backpack, and tosses it along with hers onto the sofa.

"I guess we're not finished with this place, yet."

I nod, and we head out the front door. When we are a block from our destination, Annie squeezes my hand. "Good luck."

We'll both need all the luck we can get. With no plan, and no idea how this will go, I continue. There wasn't time to come up with one. Even if we had miraculously thought up something, there is just no way to know what Alexandre will do. I no longer understand him. I don't even know what I will do when I see him. Will I murder the man, or give up? I feel equally inclined to either stab him in the heart, or just go back to bed. Eternity is exhausting enough, without adding heart-wrenching drama into the mix.

Rounding the corner, I see him. A man I love dearly, not romantically, but with loyal and undying friendship. Instead of feeling intense anger, I feel deep sadness. I am mourning the loss of two men--one my love, one my friend. I want to stop and turn around, I am just so tired. But, I won't stop, I won't turn around. Instead, I keep walking, our eyes locked, until I am standing an arm's length away.

There is no sparkle in his eye, no gleam of perfect white teeth as he smiles, no charm, and no playful banter. We are as if strangers to each other. How many times can a heart break? I refuse to be the first one to speak, so I stand mute, hands clasped in front of me, attempting to look as relaxed as possible. Alexandre looks me in the eye, but his hands are in his pockets, his shoulders slumped.

"I still have him."

"You mean, he's alive?" I try to keep my voice as calm, as possible.

"He's alive, for now."

"What is this, Alexandre? Just tell me what I have to do."

"I will release him, on the condition you never see him again. You will not turn him."

"Surely, you don't think that I can be with you after all this? Not even as companions. You are beyond delusional."

"No, I'm not crazy, Mills. I expect you to leave, for now. But, Jack will live out his mortal life without you. When he is gone, perhaps one day, we can put all this behind us. You always talk about how alone you are. Did you ever consider how it made me feel? You haven't been alone in two hundred forty years, I made sure of that."

He is both right and wrong. He is crazy, deeply, if he thinks time will make any difference. But, I now see what I have done to him, how I have hurt him. I begin to feel optimistic. Alexandre can be as looney as he wants, as long as I can get Jack away from him. I pause, to let Alexandre think I need time to ponder this offer.

"Agreed. But, I want to see him, and tell him."

Alexandre rolls his eyes. "There is no need for you two to see each other. I will send Jack on his way. Don't forget you tried to trick me once before with Julien."

"First, I need confirmation he's alive. Second, Jack will never leave me unless I make him. I'm too tired of all this to try and trick you. I just want this over and Jack safe."

Alexandre shuffles his feet. He doesn't want to take me, but I know he wants this nightmare to end as badly as I do, so I push him a little.

"I'm tired, Alexandre. I want this over with, as much as you do."

"Fine. I don't want to hurt you, Mills, but I think you know now, what I am capable of. This goes beyond loving you, you belong to me, and always will. Convince him to leave, and then we can all move on."

The last bit makes me wince. No longer will I be under any man's thumb. I choose my destiny. But I agree, at least outwardly. Alexandre tells me where they have been hiding; an abandoned plantation house about an hour up the coast.

"Alexandre, did you kill Kathryn Hart?"

He looks at me for a moment that is too long, and I know.

"I really didn't mean to. She was crazy, unhinged, and drunk. *Very drunk*. I simply pushed her away, and when she fell, she broke her neck. It was an accident."

He looks down, like he is contrite, but I know he is lying. Kathryn Hart was strangled, and he did it. He didn't push her off him, he squeezed the life from her. How have I never seen the truth? I have truly been a blind fool, in so many ways.

"Let's just go," I say, trying to hide my disgust.

We take off, alongside each other, for the first time in a while. Annie has remained successfully hidden, and I know she will follow. I wish I could communicate with her, but if I try to send her any sort of message, I will open her up to Alexandre.

One of Annie's many qualities is her ability to think on her feet, a skill she honed during what she calls "The War". She is an asset in the fight I know is coming. There is no way in hell I will go along with Alexandre's asinine plan. As I feel, now more than ever, he has lost it. We may have a shot.

Alexandre, himself, told me once about a very ancient vampire he knew. One of the only times, he ever told me about another immortal. This vampire had been alive for so long, he snapped. Before ending his own existence, he took out several of his immortal children. I never understood why crazy people feel the need to take others with them. It would be great if they would just off themselves and be done with it. There is no hope for Alexandre, and no hope for us if we don't help him with his exit. I will kill him or die trying.

When Alexandre and I stop, we stand in the middle of an oak lined, gravel road, facing a derelict, but still beautiful plantation house. I usually love these sorts of settings, but I'm not inclined to look around too much.

With my superhuman hearing, I can hear Jack laboring to breathe, inside. I start to move up the road, but Alexandre puts his hand on my arm.

"Remember what you said, *child*. Don't break your word to me."

My anger wells up, but I manage to politely incline my head.

Reaching the front door, which looks as if it is hanging on by a thread, my maker gallantly holds it open for me, as if all we are doing is going to see a movie. Jack is sitting on the floor, slumped against the wall, in the front parlor. He sees me, tries to stand, but instead takes a sharp intake of breath, holding his side.

"Don't get up," I say, and run to him.

He looks like he's been through the ringer, through gritted teeth, I say to Alexandre, "Was this necessary?"

"He tried to escape." Is all he says, as if this explains everything.

No matter, I think, my blood will heal him. He will never feel pain again.

"Shall I leave you, to say your goodbyes? I suppose I could grant you some privacy." His smugness is off the charts.

"Goodbyes?" Jack manages to croak out.

"Don't worry, it will all be over, soon."

I kiss Jack on his mouth. I'm over being passive. I may want to be with Jack, but he will never rule me. No man will ever rule me again.

"Mills," begins Alexandre.

But, I don't give him time to finish his stupid thought. Instead I move like lightening, hitting him with the full force of my body, like a freight train, pushing him backward into the decaying staircase. Alexandre flies through the air and hits it hard. Old wood splinters and falls all around him. I know this was the only chance I had to catch him off guard. It wasn't good enough, not by a long shot.

Before he can right himself, I am on top of him. Grabbing his head on either side I start bashing the back of his head into the solid hardwood floor. If I can destroy his brain, or remove his head, I'm in business. After about three good bangs, he manages to push his legs up and kicks me hard in the gut, sending me flying through the glass window next to the door.

I can only imagine what all this looks like to Jack. I also wonder where my sidekick is. Now would be a great time to show up. I hit the front porch railing, then tumble onto the grass, which feels so soft and cool. I am bleeding from multiple areas, but I have no time to think about it, or even stand up, before Alexandre is on me.

He straddles me. I feel his full weight, as he grips my throat and tries to pop off my head. Fighting for all I am worth, I feel the skin at the base of my neck beginning to tear, he is close to success. Starting to panic, I can see Annie. I know she has finally chosen her moment. She takes up a large portion of railing and hits Alexandre square in the side of the head.

He rolls off me as I raggedly force myself to stand. Alexandre is just too fast, he is up again, taking Annie up like a rag doll, hurtling her body against the solid trunk of an ancient oak tree. I know she isn't dead, but her temporarily broken body falls to the ground, unconscious.

I may die here, but I really want to take Alexandre with me. The roof of the porch looks extremely unstable, but I need higher ground. I leap up, over Alexandre's head. I almost fall but manage to right myself. Alexandre's face is bloody. He looks up at me, smiling in a very creepy way, blood dripping down his long fangs.

"You have no chance, and I can't possibly let any of you live after this."

"What a statement to smile about, killing your own children, your own creations."

"You gave me no choice, Millicent! It could have been so different, so beautiful!"

"There is nothing beautiful about you, Alexandre. At least if I die, I'll be rid of you, once and for all."

His smile vanishes. With almost no effort, he jumps onto the roof next to me. Our combined weight is too much for the ancient boards to handle, and soon we are crashing through. As luck would have it, or perhaps thanks to gravity as I am lighter, I fall last, right on top of Alexandre's back. I'm not strong enough to rip off his head by myself, and the only other way to kill him is to set him on fire or wait for the sun. None of which I can do at the moment. I go back to trying to bash his head, ramming it into the ancient wood of the porch, trying desperately not to let him out from under me.

When I feel like I can hold on no longer, Jack yells, "Hold him down, and duck your head!"

Alexandre tries bucking me off, but I hold him down with sheer force of will. The rusty ax Jack is wielding comes down with strong surety and removes Alexandre's head from his body.

CHAPTER TWENTY-THREE

Jack drops to his knees beside Alexandre's lifeless body. We just look at each other, both exhausted. There are a million things to say and no way in which to say them. We've won, I can't quite believe it. I push myself up, leaving Jack. I need to get to Annie. She is just beginning to stir, when I reach her. I gather her up in my arms.

"We're alive. How did that happen?" *Still able to keep things light, this is a good sign.*

"You saved me from having my head popped like a champagne cork. You bought us the time we needed, for me to fight Alexandre, and for Jack to save the day."

"Sweet, so I'm the hero. You can thank me after you help me up."

We stand with our arms around each other and walk back to Jack, who is still kneeling next to Alexandre. Annie and I look at our maker. I know what she is feeling, because I am feeling it too.

"I wish it could have been different." Her voice cracks.

I couldn't agree more. If only he could have been who I thought he was. Jack finds a rusted shovel and a spade, in the same dilapidated shed where the ax came from. I tell him to sit down, he is still human, and in worse shape than us. Besides, this is for Alexandre's children, *alone*.

We dig a hole, next to a stream, behind the property. When Alexandre has been placed inside and covered up again, we sit next to him in silence. I find myself overcome with emotion. Annie and I hold each other as we cry over a friend who was once so dear. We don't speak any words over his make shift grave. What would we say? Grief like a heavy blanket, more smothering than the thick, humid air, settles over me.

With dawn approaching once more, we know we aren't going to make it back home, or to any other shelter we could trust. This place seems abandoned enough. We find a root cellar to serve as our accommodations for the day. Jack volunteers to do his best to keep watch from above. He hasn't had any food or water, but insists he'll live one more night.

When it is time for Annie and me to descend, Jack takes my hand, and kisses the knuckles. We have yet to have a conversation. I suppose now we know we have all the time in the world ahead of us, there is no rush.

"I'm so sorry, Millicent," he says to me.

"I'm sorry, too. Sorry he chose this ending."

Annie and I make ourselves as comfortable as possible. God knows what is down here. I try not to think about it, as we curl up next to each other and black out with the rising sun.

I wake to something licking my neck, which isn't pleasant, since I'm positive it's a rat. The poor thing never has a chance, I'm famished. Annie and I are mostly healed. This is another benefit of being a powerful, immortal being. My neck is still sore, but since it was almost dislodged from my body, it's not hard to understand why.

We decide the best course of action will be to put Jack in a taxi, while Annie and I return home the same way we came. The two of us look the worse for wear, covered in dried blood. Our clothing is in tatters. Best to avoid humans, if it all possible.

We beat Jack to the house and clean ourselves up. We manage to fill our bellies on the way. Our triumph isn't feeling very triumphant.

After my shower, I knock on Annie's bedroom door. She says to come in, and when I do, I find her in tears at her vanity. I've seen more vampire tears in the last forty-eight hours, then I have in over two hundred years of life.

"I don't feel very good about what happened, Mills."

I sit down on the bed. "Neither do I. How can we feel good about going against Alexandre? But, all you did was save me, you didn't lastingly hurt him. If that helps."

She doesn't answer. It will take us all time to get over the events of last night. As it turns out, Alexandre was a monster, but he was also our maker, our family, and that means something. Was he a monster before I knew him? Or was it loving me that ruined him? These questions will haunt me.

"Where will you go?" I ask my only friend in the world.

"Somewhere far away. I need to distance myself. Will you sell the house?"

"First chance I get. Everything will be put in storage, so don't worry about leaving your things behind. I'll take care of them." I pause, needing a moment to keep my emotions in check. "When will we see you again?"

"Soon, I promise. You and Jack will need time, too."

"I'm holding you to it."

"Annie, one more thing. Do you think we should have buried the head somewhere else?"

"What are you talking about?"

"We know so little about ourselves. All we know about our nature and powers, we learned from Alexandre. We have come to find out that he hasn't always been truthful, about a lot of things."

"That's putting it mildly," she says.

After a few minutes of contemplation, Annie adds, "I don't know. Losing your head seems pretty final. This isn't a movie. Do you want to go back and move it? We can, if it will make you feel better."

"No, you're right. This isn't a movie. I can't imagine how he could still live," I reason.

"Agreed. Let's leave Alexandre in peace."

Annie pulls herself together, re-gathers her things, and leaves. Ever the independent, she needs to go off on her own now. I completely understand, I wouldn't have her any other way. By the time Jack arrives, I am more than ready to put Savannah in the rear-view mirror myself.

Taking a breather, we sit on the loveseat in my beautiful living room. There is still blood from the tears of two vampires on one side, but I don't care. Jack stretches his arm around my shoulders and pulls me to him. I relax against his chest. I can't quite believe everything that happened. I try to tell myself it was all worth it, I now have what I always wanted. However, the ghosts of Kathryn Hart and Alexandre, will forever lurk in the background. While he was a monster, there was so much more to him.

"How are you feeling, Millicent?" Jack asks, breathing into my hair.

"I'm ok. I'll be ok."

"Yes, you will. We have a lot to do, with all the time in the world to do it. We'll go slow, and we'll heal."

I hold him tighter. Sitting on that bloodstained loveseat, we make plans for our future.

We'll travel to London, so Jack can close out his life. There are bank accounts, a house, and a career he will formally retire from. As soon as he is ready, we will find a small isolated place, far away from the world. A place with a room for Annie. I think of Alexandre's little cottage in the French woods, wondering if it's still there. Disappearing won't be easy for a man with a familiar face, but time will help us.

I am interested in researching our origins. Finding out, if I can, where we came from and especially how Alexandre came into his immortality. I have known other immortals briefly. Never have I bothered to ask about our origins, or Alexandre's mysterious "ways". I have been apathetic for so long. It feels as if I am waking up from a long nap, no longer content just to exist and pass the time.

Once we have disappeared, I will share immortality with Jack and my life will begin, in earnest. Jack isn't unsure or nervous, one bit. This is his destiny as much as it was mine. He is ready to move into another realm of life. And what a life, it will be.

COMING IN 2019- BOOK TWO in the IMMORTAL KINDRED SERIES

REBEL HEART

Chapter 1

The ground was frozen, slick with mud. My hands, tied to a pole behind my back, were tingling with lack of circulation. I knew I was in a tent. It was so dark when I came to, I couldn't see anything. Still, I knew.

Cold water steadily dripped onto my shoulder from above. My head throbbed where someone had hit me from behind. A trickle of liquid was oozing its way down my forehead, past my temple. Logic would tell me I have been captured by the English or the even more hated Hessians. Attempting to still my breathing, I concentrated on listening. Outside, I heard muffled voices, along with feet slapping in and pulling out of the muddy ground.

This was my sixth assignment as a Culper Spy. I'm still not sure where it all went wrong. Something stuck, pinched in my gut, from the moment I accepted the seemingly simple assignment. Deliver a message, that was all I had to do. But, with all the key players acting shifty with a wound-up nervousness, the walls couldn't help but fall. One thing I knew for sure was, it hadn't felt right from the start.

"You should learn to listen to yourself more, Annie. Now look what's happened." I mumbled to myself, trying to work my sleeping hands behind me.

I caught a clear word from a male voice, just outside the tent.

Oh no, German. This meant one thing, I had to get the hell out of these bonds now.

CLARA WINTER

ABOUT THE AUTHOR

Amy Rugg grew up reading *Anne of Green Gables*, *The Secret Garden*, and *Alice in Wonderland*, while watching *Buck Rogers*, *Star Trek*, and *Doctor Who*. Writing her own stories naturally ensued. She is a wife, mother, and former school counselor, with a Master's Degree in Counseling. Amy is from Colorado Springs, Co and currently resides in Mission Viejo, Ca.

Connect with her at: clarawinterbooks.com

Made in the USA
San Bernardino, CA
12 August 2018